The Christmas Star

A Christmas Land Story

Marcel Ortiz

The Christmas Star

October 2012

This book is a work of fiction. Names, characters, places, and incidents either are products of the author's imagination or are used fictitiously. Any resemblance to actual events, locales, or persons, living or dead, is entirely coincidental.

Copyright © 2012 by Marcel Ortiz

All rights reserved, including the right of reproduction in whole or in part in any form.

ISBN: 1480107883

ISBN-13: 978-1480107885

Welcome to Christmas Land!

A land where Christmas is eagerly anticipated all year. Where Saint Nicholas, also known as Santa Claus resides with his reindeer and sleigh, making toys for all the good girls and boys with the help of Elves.

Sereen has been raised by the cruel Witch Nyriee for as long as she can remember; tormented and forced to work as little better than a slave.

Then one day a King's messenger arrives, bearing news that the Prince has been issued an ultimatum by his father. He has until Christmas, a bare four months away, to choose a bride.

But all does not go as planned once Nyriee, her daughters, Areenie and Floria, and Sereen arrive at the Christmas Palace. And soon Sereen is in danger, far greater than she even knows.

Nyriee wants to marry off one of her poor daughters to the Prince.

But as Sereen interferes with her plans she decides to remove the threat... Interfering with another's plans...

Dedicated To:

My Family

May you never stop believing

in the Magic of Christmas

Oh, Christmas Star

You lit the way to Bethlehem far

Your good pure light

Lit the way through the darkest night

Let your light shine on…

Prologue 1

"You have failed Luce!" Laughter tinkled in the voice as it echoed in the silence.

He growled into the night, searching with a dark fire in his eyes, searching for the owner of the voice. His voice was dark, throbbing with power as he called into the night.

"Come out, come out wherever you are."

It should have been a croon meant to lure and lull, instead it was a dark command, lending a hint to his true nature.

"Tsk, tsk, Luce, I would have expected better of you." A second voice danced through the night.

Violently, he spun in circles hunting, hunting for the owners of those pure and tinkling voices, filled with laughter and light that tormented him ceaselessly.

He stilled when one of the voices whispered in his ear, as if she was standing right there, "You can't find us Luce, you've fallen too far."

He didn't even bother trying to turn, instead stood there for a second longer. The owner of that voice would have already moved by the time he'd tried to grab her.

"Maybe not as far as we'd thought." He could almost see the answering nod.

His voice was rife with dark intent as he shouted, "You forget, I'm not so dumb as those before."

"Ahh, but Luce you've already proven you're not the angel you were once thought to be."

A vicious snarl curled his lips as he stared menacingly into the night. "Just because one opportunity has passed me by, do not believe I cannot find others."

"Oh, Luce. It is already too late. You are stuck in Christmas Land, tied here, permanently."

He smiled evilly into the dark. "You forget, there is a way out."

An image formed in front of him. A beautiful woman pale as new fallen snow, and behind her another, with black hair highlighted with darkest purple. They spoke in harmony, identical looks of horror on their faces.

"You would not dare, Luce, you wouldn't!"

"You would not harm such an innocent creature!"

He sneered at them, "You forget that I know what lies on the other side if I find and claim the Christmas Star. I know the power."

They shook their heads, sorrow and grief mixed on their faces. "You were once great Luce, so great as to defy all meaning, but you forget the Christmas Star will not just be taken and claimed. You must give reason for it to agree, to agree to your claim."

"You think I cannot do it?" He glowered at the images, already knowing they weren't corporeal. "Wait and see, my dear Queens, I will possess the Christmas Star, wait and see."

They started to fade, still shaking their heads. "Luce, you were once a brave and noble Angel, but in this you will fail. No Star is owned by any, except those they love, and no Star would find love with your tainted heart."

He glowered at the two them as they faded into a sparkling mist, then out of sight. "I will find the Christmas Star, have no doubts about that!"

Their combined voices echoed throughout the hollow where he'd fallen after his attempt to destroy God's son. "We have little doubt you shall find her, the question remains how shall you convince her?"

Prologue II

A loud cry echoed up and down the hollow from the cottage nestled so peacefully in the snow, blending flawlessly into the scene around it. The snow glittered like diamonds under the moon's stunning light as it surrounded the little cottage.

It was a newborn babe's cry that wrent the cold night's air.

All the creatures in the hollow stopped and stared intently at the cottage. The chittering of squirrels and the soft chirping of birds echoed through the night as they spoke rapidly to each other. This birth had been long awaited and now all were curious about this newborn creature.

What creatures could, went to those upstairs windows and peered in, hoping for a sight of that precious bundle.

Inside the warm and glowing cottage an exhausted mother held a swaddled babe in her arms. The doting father stood protectively over her and the babe.

In a moonbeam, shining brightly through the window dancing sparkles appeared. The animals were taken back for a moment then stared intently at the entrancing shimmers. Outlines were being formed by the shimmering sparkles. Slowly, they formed bodies. The Queens of the Fairies had come to see this precious child.

Christabel, Queen of the Snowflake Fairies and Berry, Queen of the Sugar Plum Fairies, stood in the humble cottage, as regal as their titles. They were two of the most powerful beings in Christmas Land, second only to the King. Apart they were powerful, but together they were a force that was to be feared, but only by those with evil intentions.

They were stunning to gaze upon. Christabel with her pure white form, glittering subtly as she moved; Berry with her pale skin, black hair shimmering with deepest purple highlights, and a rustling dress of deepest maroon, shedding sparkling dust as she moved.

The baby was the first to notice the Fairies that had come to visit. It giggled and gestured towards them, bringing smiles to their faces such as to melt hearts. If the animals had been more as the Elfen they would have fallen in love with them right there, forever worshipping. As it was they were already in love with them. They loved them as all animals were raised to love such benevolent and powerful creatures that ruled the wild.

Man and woman looked up and stared, shocked at the creatures of such beauty before them. They both loved them, but they were also deeply in love themselves, being soul mates of the truest kind. Both bowed their heads in acknowledgment of the beings before them. The Queens inclined their heads and stepped forward.

With ever so gentle hands Christabel reached for the child, nestling her close. The parents gave her reluctantly, with twin concerned looks, despite the sure knowledge nothing would harm her in the Fairies' care, they watched as the Fairies smiled down at their babe. Huge purple eyes blinked up at them, innocence in its truest form.

"She will be great one day." Berry looked up, directing her intense maroon gaze at them. "What shall you name her?"

There would be great importance in her name. The creatures waited in hushed silence for the answer. It took several moments of deep thought before the parents brought forth a name—but such a fitting name it was.

"Sereen, we shall name her Sereen." A name fit for a Star.

The Fairies shared a knowing look with each other. Their forms shimmering, with—something. Berry looked down at the child, speaking in a voice that sounded like the sweetest candy, "Such a name little one. Little Sereen."

"You will be great one day Sereen, such purity in you." Intoned Christabel with an aura of prophecy to her voice.

Christabel raised the child up, letting the swaddling blanket fall off. Much to the astonishment of the animals and her parents, they saw her dressed in a dress of purest shimmering white, as if it was encrusted in diamonds, a silver circlet adorning her brow. Then her entire form shimmered and changed, she became older, a young woman of such beauty that she rivaled even the

Fairies in her splendor, in a different, less obvious way, glowing with some inner radiance.

The vision faded as Christabel handed the babe back to her anxious parents, who immediately looked their child over to make sure was nothing wrong, though they knew the Fairies had done naught. "She will be great one day. Love her well."

The parents thanked both Fairies profusely for coming offering them food, drink, whatever they desired, within reason, but the Fairies refused, leaving the parents with their tiny child. Telling them instead to enjoy the time with their daughter.

***

As they stood outside they gazed back at the cottage. Their footsteps already hidden by the snow.

In a voice layered with sadness Christabel spoke. "It shall be a hard life for that tiny one."

"Yes, but if she lives to the promise whispered beneath the skin, perhaps she can save all that has or could be lost, to him."

Christabel gave Berry a sad smile, "She will have a hard life before her, many things to turn such a magnificent heart cold."

"We shall both hope." Berry's smile was fraught with a dark understanding.

They looked towards the shadows of a large tree where a deer and other, smaller, creatures had crept close to see them. Further down there were three wolves, their eyes refracting light, glowing in their eerie way.

They stopped short and gestured the animals forward after sharing a look.

The animals flocked around them, keeping a careful distance from them, in awe of these creatures.

Berry spoke in gentle tones, the undercurrent of command threading itself through. She gestured broadly towards the cottage.

"As you already know, tonight a shining star was born, a bright creature sent to us. We must protect her as if she is more important than our young, our hides. To keep her safe from ones who would seek her destroyed or enslaved." Berry's eyes flashed fire despite the gentle tone and the animals understood, taking her meaning to heart. "Keep close watch of her my friends and guard her well." And perhaps Christmas Land will finally become what it once was.

In a whirl of maroon skirts and hair she walked towards Christabel and in a flash of shimmers they disappeared.

The animals stared after them until the last of the cloud of brilliance was gone, then they turned back towards the house, to watch the happy scene.

Late that night they called a formal court and decided amongst themselves they would watch over her. Keeping care of her both near and far. Ordering that all creatures would be informed of their duty to her and of her existence. For they'd all seen in that image, the truth, the undeniable fact that despite her form she was a Star, belonging to them and them to her and, until she could protect herself, she was their charge.

Beneath the full moon they took a solemn vow to guard and protect the Christmas Star.

Chapter One

Sereen opened her eyes slowly, the first sight greeting her eyes in the dawn's early light was that of several forest creatures nestled in front of and beside her, a common sight in the morning. They'd been doing this for as long as she could remember. Chipmunks and squirrels nestling together in a pile of soft fur, breathing in unison. With a sigh she pushed herself up, rubbing her arms as the frigid air attacked her and started working on laying a fire on the cold hearth. Birds and other creatures, earlier risers, ran back and forth bringing her the kindling and helping her get the fire started. Their energy was endless it seemed and as they sang their morning songs they infected her with their cheer. Often as not they were what kept her going in the morning.

The sun was barely tingeing the sky purple as she went to work on breakfast. All too soon the three of them would be up, pushing and demanding. She started the giant hot water vat boiling, preparing it for the inevitable baths. Today all three of them would bathe, as would she, but only after those three were done and in bed for the night. It was difficult to do anything during the day with those three constantly demanding. And she never knew when she'd have a task to complete that involved getting filthy.

Taking a moment for herself, she stared outside at the splendor that surrounded her. It was rare during the day for her to have an opportunity to take a break, she'd learned to take whatever brief moments she could and enjoy what life offered. The new morning sun made the snow gleam as if it was made up of diamonds, instead of ice crystals. Everything was covered in a fresh layer of snow, the leaves starting their slow descent off the trees. It created an interesting contrast between the reds and greens and the snow itself.

Winter had set in early this year. Mid August had seen the snow. The crops had been difficult to get in. It appeared for those that didn't have plenty of riches there'd be a lean winter, but there'd been a lot of lean winters. The food shortage meant nothing to those peacefully resting above stairs, it didn't even affect her, but she always took notice and helped where she could.

One of the fawns tentatively walked over to her, butting her leg, she laughed, rubbing its head. This one hadn't been in this world long and it wobbled some as it sought her fingers. After several minutes the chill started to seep in. Giving the fawn one last rub she went into the house to start breakfast.

Morning was the time for herself, doing as she wished with no threat of repercussions. The Ladies slept late most mornings and even then didn't leave their rooms for hours. Part of the morning routine was clanging pots together and general misbehaving, that otherwise wouldn't be tolerated. Little things that she could see or remember during the day and bring a smile to her face.

She looked up with a start when a bell rang.

At first she thought it was one of the three ringing their bells, it was early for one of them to be awake, but stranger things had happened. She'd just started getting the trays together when the bell rang again. The animals stopped chattering from their perches and she realized with an odd sense of foreboding it was the front bell.

She dashed towards the front door, curiosity burning through her, along with a dark shudder. It had to be something imperative if someone was up this early. Their closest neighbor was several hours away, and as far as she knew, none of them would bother coming around here. Despite her best attempts she couldn't put away the shudder that ran down her spine.

A gust of wind and snow entered as she opened the door and invited the person in. The snow blinded her for an instant and she blinked it away as she pushed the door closed.

Barely, she kept her mouth from gaping open, shocked as she stared at the man before her. He was dressed in the red and white candy striping of a King's Messenger. He stood ramrod straight and he spoke just as stiffly. It was obvious he'd been on quite a trip, though not enough to take the starch out of his breeches.

"Are you the Lady of the house? Lady Nyriee Dantaan?"

Sereen shook her head then remembered that it was rude. It was so easy to be informal. "No, I'm not. My Lady is still abed."

He gave her a once over, as if saying, 'of course you aren't the mistress, I was merely attempting to be polite.' She felt her cheeks heat with embarrassment at the disdainful look, as if he could tell she had no family. He handed her a letter, addressed to the Lady Nyriee

Dantaan in gold lettering. The letter looked rich, something befitting the King of Christmas Land.

"Give this to your Lady Dantaan." His tone implied he doubted she was to be trusted with anything so important as the letter she held. But as there was no one he else he would be forced to give it to her.

"Of course." Woodenly she nodded at him.

Briefly she contemplated asking him if he would like to rest for a moment, maybe have something to drink, despite his disdain, but he was already gone, a gust of wind blowing through the now open door. It figured that he wouldn't even close the door behind him.

Sereen turned away shaking her head, quickly closing the door behind him. Somehow Nyriee always knew when the temperature dropped the slightest amount. Heaving a great sigh she looked at her dress, her general appearance. It seemed perfectly acceptable to her. Nothing was out of place. Her dress may have been getting a little worn, but it was clean. There was nothing that had warranted treating her like a vagabond, or a thief. Starting back towards the kitchen she almost dropped the letter before she remembered it was in her hand.

Staring down at the letter she contemplated, it would be easy to make it disappear to make that messenger right, but what if Nyriee was expecting it? What she really needed to do was go up and give it to her. Sometimes she wished she could read letters without opening them, if it was good news she should take it right up, because the consequences would be little or none, if it was bad... Taking a deep breath she mounted the steps to the bedrooms.

Running her hand along the cool wood of the banister she relished its bite, wishing it were snow.

Often times she'd run ice over the banister, smoothing the wood, wiping off the grease that accumulated. The landing was cold, but not in a heating manner. Just as all the rest of the house, it told you to stand back, you weren't welcome. Even its inhabitants felt unwanted, like intruders.

Once she'd tried to bring some welcoming warmth to the house, never again, not in that manner. She'd made minor changes, but never such a large one again. The scars from the lashes still showed in stark relief against her pale skin. They'd been deep and painful, so much so that her every movement had been agony, but it had been complete her workload or get another. The animals had saved her, banding around her, doing as much as they could and placing salves on her back as often as was needed. They'd saved her life, making sure no infection set into the scabbed wounds.

The door's handle was icy under her palm, much like its mistress. She rested her forehead against the chilly door and strengthened her resolve—

"You might as well come in." The voice was piercing, musical in the manner of a sour note, too high held too long.

Nyriee always knew, Sereen had long ago decided that the woman had powers that her daughters knew nothing of, not that Areenie and Floria would have noticed if she'd shouted it at them. Unless it was something like money, a dress, or something that directly impacted them they couldn't lower themselves to notice.

The room was pitch black, if she hadn't spent so many hours cleaning and learning her bearings she would have run into several things on her way to the curtains. Finally finding them she pulled one side open letting in the warm, golden sunlight. It barely pierced the gloom, but it was enough.

Nyriee was sitting up against her headboard, black silk surrounding her. Sereen stopped a moment to take in how old she was starting to look. Wrinkles were forming, her hair graying, her general appearance was old. She'd never remark upon it to Nyriee, to even think such a thing would get her in trouble if she was found out.

"Stop standing there gawking, what is it?" Her voice cut like razors, forcing her into action. She held out the letter.

"This letter just came by Royal Messenger for you, milady."

She snatched it up, "I see." Then pretended nonchalance. For several moments Sereen continued to stand there while her mistress turned the letter this way and that. Her gaze seemed to go right through Sereen when she zeroed back in on her. "Well? What are you still doing here? Go and get my breakfast."

Panic coursed through her for a second as she turned away, not even bothering to give a 'yes, milady,' breakfast was surely burned!

***

Mercifully breakfast was not burned, it was perfectly done. The animals had pitched in and gotten it off without even a singed hair, which had happened before. She thanked them all profusely as she started putting the trays together.

They all insisted on being served in their rooms, heaven forbid they come downstairs so early in the day. It meant more work for her, not that they'd ever consider or care. It had been this way for all her eighteen years and she saw no hope for a change now. Taking a deep breath she let it out slowly, trying to get rid of all her angry thoughts. There was nothing she could do about it, so why be angry about it? It helped, some, mostly it calmed her erratic heart.

She almost dumped the tray when Nyriee's voice pierced the hall. "GIRLS! Come here NOW!"

Wincing she continued to make her way towards Nyriee's room, now she was going to have to get their trays as well. Two doors banged shut in the hall and she just saw Areenie and Floria disappearing into their mother's bedroom. Instead of calling out for them to hold the door she waited until the door had snicked shut. After a brief rap on the door she entered.

Both girls were sitting with their legs folded under them staring up at their mother, who was waving the letter around. It bore all of the kingdom's colors of red, white, green, and gold. From where she was it looked like some type of notice, of what she was curious. With any luck it wouldn't be anything bad, like they were getting thrown in the dungeon. The Christmas Palace wasn't supposed to have one, but stories claimed it did, for the most vile of Elfen. Or one could be thrown into the Tundra, where those that were unacceptable and could never fit into society were sent.

The Tundra was a stark, barren wasteland, only those completely incapable of being part of society were sent out there. And only on the most rare of occasions were those sent out there ever seen again. Though supposedly there were those that went willingly to the Tundra, those that didn't wish to be around normal society, they were few and far between.

Walking slowly she made her way to place the tray on the table, hoping to overhear as much of the conversation as she could. Any information could prove beneficial. Sometimes the difference of being whipped or not, was being prepared, overhearing that key conversation where things were decided.

"Girls, the most impressing news has just been made known to me. The Prince is on the hunt for a wife!" The girls gasped, shocked, it surprised Sereen as well. As far as she'd knew the Prince was a scapegrace, rumors spoke that he was a shameless lady's man, and his father was out of things to do with him. Since his wife's death the King hadn't been right, according to what she'd heard, despite the fact it had been over a hundred years ago. He'd never recovered and apparently his son had gone wild after her death, becoming an unbearable menace.

As of late the rumors had been getting worse. She turned away anymore from the rumors, not wanting to believe that someone that should be respected, and was by many, and held such power would misuse it in such ways.

"'To show support for the Prince's quest he's decided to invite eligible Ladies to the court and present themselves, thus increasing the chance of his son to find a suitable wife. And—" She flapped her hands, excitement raising her already high voice higher. "It says here the Prince is to marry on Christmas Eve. Can you imagine? A wedding at the Christmas Palace before the entire court." Her voice had taken on a wistful quality, lost in the picture she'd painted for herself.

If she wants to marry the Prince herself she's going to need to reverse the aging process. Sereen almost laughed at the thought, Nyriee being younger. Nyriee was stunningly beautiful, even with her age. With her ice blue eyes and silver-white hair, she must have been something to behold in her youth. If she'd tried to woo the Prince then undoubtedly she would have won him, there was little doubt of that in Sereen's mind. No, it was up to her ungainly daughters to win him, neither of which, it seemed to Sereen, had the wiles or poise to do so.

Nyriee's loud voice, drowning out the tittering of her daughters jolted Sereen back from her reverie. "We must pack immediately, the sooner we leave the sooner we catch a Prince!"

Sereen ducked out before Nyriee realized she was still there.

***

The rest of the day was spent on washing, folding, and packing. While the girls discussed what court would be like and what dresses would best display their stunning selves Sereen ran herself ragged, trying to complete an enormous task without help. She'd often wondered why Nyriee had no other servants. It was obvious there was more than enough in the coffers, no expense was ever spared.

Just as twilight had taken over the sky, she was called to Nyriee's rooms. Nyriee needed a coach to carry herself, her daughters, and the luggage. The only person suitable for the task of getting one was Sereen, who was ready to fall over, dead on her feet. So as night finished descending over the land, she put on the heaviest cloak she owned, a thin and thread bare thing, and prepared to go out into the frozen night. She grabbed a lantern and shut the door firmly behind herself. The plan was she'd make the arrangements for the coach and return home, then the day after tomorrow the coach would arrive and take them to the Palace, where the Prince would fall insanely in love with one of Nyriee's daughters, both in their perfect dresses, and they'd all live happily ever after.

Hopefully far, far away.

Like as not she'd freeze to death and they'd never make it to the Palace proper. She was slightly curious as to what they would do with her. It briefly crossed her mind that they would kill her, removing all evidence of their previous lives, but she decided that it wasn't very likely. After all if they failed it wouldn't do to have blood on their hands, they would be out a servant-slave.

In the distance the house was just disappearing when the animals came out. Deer, reindeer, and all manner of other creatures, walked behind her until she started shivering. One of the reindeer nudged her in the back, and then knelt, bowing its head. Rubbing between his antlers, she showed her thanks and climbed on his back. The snow was thick and with no snow shoes going was difficult at best.

They continued on their way for a while before she started shivering in earnest, much to her surprise something warm and furry was draped over her shoulders. Instead of questioning the gift, she hunkered down to her reindeer as they continued into the night.

Some time into the journey it started to snow intensely, showing the real fury of a storm. Instead of stopping the animals moved closer to her and several small, well-heated, furry bodies ended up under her cloak. And in the mesmerizing view of the storm she fell asleep, her face pressed to a silky coat.

A cold nose pressing insistently against her neck woke her up. Around her was darkness, but as her eyes focused she noticed a light in the distance. Taking the warm body in her hand she sat upright, surprised at how rested she felt. It was the best sleep she'd had in a long while.

As they drew closer she gently pulled on the fur around the reindeer's neck, urging him to a stop. Coming to a halt she slid off his back, landing daintily on her feet. Thanking all the animals profusely she walked up to the Inn. Carefully she rubbed snow in her dress to make it look like she'd actually walked. Despite the abundance of magic in the land it still would have looked strange to someone for her to have come the distance she had in a blizzard and have a dry skirt.

Brushing her hair back into a haphazard bun she shed the cloak she wore, handing it mournfully back to the animals, sorry to give up its generous warmth. With as bright a smile as she could muster she went towards the door of the Inn. Reaching out she rapped gently on the door, unsure if anyone would still be awake at this hour, though she wasn't sure how late it actually was.

To her surprise the door creaked open, showing the warm face of the Innkeeper's wife, Miriam. She opened the door wider and Sereen hurried in, thankful that she'd been awake.

The Inn was warm against her chilled cheeks. It was a good thing she hadn't had to walk, she probably would be lying out there now, dead. She had very few illusions about the feelings of Nyriee and her daughters, but this had been a new low, not even thinking of the weather, or her exhaustion.

A bright fire burned, giving light and warmth, tables were set up in the common room. Here and there were men eating, drinking, some were talking. A large clock stood prominently placed, telling her it was nowhere near so late as she though. They'd made good time.

"Come here dearie, let me take that for ye. That's a long walk for ye. Let's get ye all warmed up sweetie, ye hold on luv."

Sereen shook her head, smiling delightedly as the older woman bustled around. She didn't notice the stunning effect it had on everyone in the room, particularly the man standing by the fire. There weren't many people in the Inn with the cold weather outside, but there were enough they'd be doing some business tonight. Miriam returned bringing food and drink which Sereen gladly accepted. She spent the next several minutes warming up. And as she did a pleasant tiredness blanketed her, until she could barely keep her eyes open. It was the tired of warmth and comfort lulling to rest.

"Oh, luv. Your dealin's they can wait 'till t'morrow can't they?"

She kept enough of her faculties to nod and allow herself to be led away to a small cot in the back room the Innkeepers always kept open for servants that were sent on errands, since they rarely had money to pay for their own lodging. It had been an embarrassing ordeal the first time she'd been sent to the Inn and they'd inquired about if she required a room and she'd realized she had no money with which to pay for one. Miriam had instantly taken notice of her plight and informed her gently that there was a pallet in the back she could use for the night. Since then Sereen had always had a soft spot for the family.

The pallet was clean and soft, smelling of something sweet. Almost the moment her head hit the pillow she was out.

***

The animals were worried, very worried. They'd not taken much issue with the Witch before, but this went too far. Whether deliberate or not, she'd sent their charge into the freezing night without an adequate fur. None of them had a doubt in their minds that if they hadn't intervened, providing fur and transport, that the female would have died. She'd been worn-out and, instead of giving her a good night's sleep, the Witch had sent her out into the night. There were many things the animals could stand, but deliberate lack of care of young was not to be tolerated.

They talked and tittered, trying to decide what to do about this problem. The most obvious choice was to kill the Witch, but that could lead to deaths, and perhaps repercussions for their charge. They had no hesitation at the thought of telling her to flee, except they didn't believe their little one would, for too many Elfin reasons. An issue they knew would cause them nothing but pain would be when she went to the Palace. It would be more difficult to take care of their precious gift, however, nothing so foolish or dangerous should be taking place at the Master Den.

Their best bet they decided would be to let her go to the Palace with the Witch, then try to get her to escape from there. For certain there were worse places to work, worse situations, and the Witch hadn't made the attempts obvious. They figured this attempt was more about neglect to think about it than intent to kill her. The Witch didn't seem to care for the girl except as a servant and therefore below her notice, this played directly into their paws. At the Palace there would be plenty of food and fur. They would be able to care for her there.

With their meeting concluded they returned to watching over the Inn. All of them aware that they'd not decided to go for the most obvious course of action, that of finding her a mate. It would be the simplest way to extract her from the Witch's clutches, but none of them wanted the responsibility or the difficulty. They were perfectly aware that her mate would have to someone special indeed and none of them could think of a single person worthy of their precious charge.

***

Nyriee glanced out the window every few seconds. Fear had settled low in her belly in a tight knot. It had seemed such a good idea, now though…He'd be here, soon, too soon. Curse him for this. The tidal of anger couldn't overwhelm her fear. It had worked in the past, but it appeared this time inescapable.

Her mistakes washed over her, burning through her. There'd been many mistakes made today, the question was how to escape the repercussions. Shift the blame? Feign ignorance? There would be no escape, he would know. Hopefully the girl was unharmed, that would mitigate much of the problem, though not her own stupidity.

Curse all. She couldn't wait to be done with him, to finally have her freedom. That desire had made her foolish and placed her plans in jeopardy, she'd been too quick of the mark. Whirling away from the window she took in the subtle disarray of her room.

Trunks were open, the wardrobe was open, clothing clearly visible. Someday it would be nice to have more servants, but then she wouldn't be repressed. A fine path she walked, so easy to drop of either side.

A man's form showed in the corner. As she watched it finished taking shape and walked out of the dark. He had the slippery feel of an eel around him, a look that bespoke of danger and something best avoided.

She curtsied low to him, showing him the deference he deserved, or thought he did. "My Lord."

He flicked his hand at her. "Rise."

She looked up from hooded eyes at him, carefully guarding her expression. His eyes flitted over her taking in her appearance as well as the scene around her. He made her feel unworthy, like all she'd accomplished wasn't worth a thing in his eyes. His silence made her nervous, made her wonder.

Luce was tall with oily looking black hair that had a high widow's peak. His face was thin, almost gaunt, with black eyes that seemed to give a glimpse to hell itself. He was slender of build, which only belied his nasty nature. Hard to believe he was one of the most dangerous creatures in Christmas Land.

"How goes the progress with the girl? Everything is well?"

"Of course my Lord, I believe she's on that cusp of readiness, another month at the most."

"Ahh, I see, so near the mark. It seems like but yesterday she was a squalling infant." His tone was eerily paternal, in a way that indicated nothing paternal in any manner.

Nyriee forced a smile to her face. One of the worst demons fallen from the heavens was before her and had a plan hinged on something she'd sent into the cold night. She adopted a maternal tone, striving to sound indulgent. "Yes, they do grow fast."

"How do your own fair? I fear I've neglected them."

Of course he hadn't, thought of her *daughters* made her want to hurl. He knew that they were subpar beings with no magic or sense of it and to complete their lacking qualities neither was comely in the least. Luce had made careful sure that the man she married would pass on none of her abilities. But had it been too much to ask for them to at least be pretty?

"They do well, both are very attentive to their lessons. They do their *father* proud."

"Hmm."

Her remark about their father did not pass him unnoticed, she was sure. When she and Luce had struck their bargain it had been with the understanding she'd go out on her own, make her own way. She'd met and courted a man with power, not so much as to attract undue notice to her, but enough to build a base off of. In her idiocy she'd believed to have found the perfect puppet for her plans, he was pliable and easily swayed. Only later, after she'd birthed two unsatisfactory daughters had she learned he'd been a plant by Luce, who'd correctly guessed what she was looking for. Where Luce had gotten him she didn't know, but he'd been perfect for *his* plans. The wretch could be forgiven she supposed, if one learned the lesson with it.

"The girl is in perfect condition and I now have a way to get close to the crown. My daughters will make me proud."

"Yes," A distracted look came over his face for a moment, then, "I grant you permission."

Nyriee gaped at him, rage firing her blood. The nerve, thinking she'd been asking permission. She hadn't been, had she? "I didn't—"

"Take good care of the girl, very soon it shall be time." He knew! It was there in his eyes, he said nothing but he knew!

He began to blend back into the shadows, leaving as he'd come, disappearing, but not before he got off his parting shot, just as she'd been relaxing.

"How will your failures ever manage to capture a Prince?"

Nyriee was left staring at the shadows, no place to direct her rage.

"Curse you Luce," She hissed, not because he was wrong, but because he was so right. "I shall try anyway."

***

Sereen woke early and helped Miriam make the morning meals for the guests. It felt good to do something to help pay the kind woman back for the bed and meals. She told her of the wishes of the Lady of the house; for a horse and carriage to be brought to front door the next day at the earliest possible hour, and that payment would be made upon safe delivery of her person to the Christmas Palace. Miriam had shaken her head and continued on with kneading her dough. Every now and again Sereen could make out words, like 'don't know what she's doing sending that girl out in blizzard' and 'cheapest woman on earth, shoulda' been born a Witch, she shoulda' and other things along a similar line. She just shook her head at the Innkeeper's mistress and went back to her own work, aware that she needed to get going.

Lurking around in the shadows all morning, watching her, was Miriam's son, Slate. He gave her the creeps something in his manner making her nervous and uncomfortable. By mid morn she was ready to leave, if only to get away from his skulking company.

She thanked Miriam and the Innkeeper, both voicing their concerns about her walking back, their intent clear, trying to get her to spend time with Slate. They even offering the use of the carriage, with Slate, she merely shook her head and politely declined. She wanted to get away from him not be alone with him for hours.

As she was just out of sight of the Inn Slate accosted her. Grabbing her about the shoulders and pushing his face an inch from hers. Her first instinct was to fight, but once she realized who it was she quit, deciding it would do no good, at least not at the moment. She settled for glaring at him and speaking in a chill voice, such as to make an Ice Queen proud.

"What do you want Slate?'"

"I want us ta' come ta' an unners'andin', got it?"

"No."

Briefly he gave her a confused look, as if he couldn't understand a simple no. "Now see here, I means ta' marry ya an' yer gonsta say aye, gets it?"

"No."

Obviously monosyllabic sentences confused the oaf. His grip was bruising and she was ready to go. He was taking precious time out of her day.

"You must ask my mistress, she's the only one that can say yea or nay. Now I must get home or she'll be angry and when I tell her the reason she'll be disinclined to accept your request."

He stared at her for several long minutes, obviously having difficulty processing her words. Finally he must have decided she agreed because he released her. "I be speakin' ta' yer mistress when th' carriage comes, an when yer me wife ye won' be workin' wie 'er no mo'."

Sereen breathed a sigh of relief as he lumbered off. That was probably the longest speech of his life and she couldn't find a single scrap of appreciation. A new kettle of fish had been opened, but she doubted Nyriee would approve the union, if she even needed to, because it would make her lose her servant-slave.

The walk back was pleasant. The storm had abated while she'd been sleeping, leaving the world blanketed in the softest covering of white. It had transformed the world into a wonderland. As always it brought a smile to her face. Animals came out to walk with her, carefully stepping along her tracks so no one could see the strange occurrence of animals and Elfin walking together. The trip went much faster than it had the night before, this time she strolled along on her own, though the animals lent her the cloak. Deciding that some exercise would be most beneficial.

She arrived back at the house after noon that day, finding the entire house in chaos. In the rooms trunks were thrown open and clothing piled haphazardly into them. Sereen groaned at the work that awaited her, thankful that she'd left when she had, if this was how bad it was now, how bad would it have been if she'd waited any longer?

Nyriee was in an odd mood, seeming almost relieve that she was back, than snapping at her the next moment.

Under her careful command the chests were repacked and the house tidied. Despite frequent pauses to cater to their whims, everything came together smoothly and efficiently. The girls made it out like it was her fault she'd been ordered to go to the Inn, while Nyriee simply had a pained expression and glared.

Falling into bed she was worn to the bone, but couldn't go to sleep. Her own meager belongings had been packed as well, though Nyriee still hadn't told her what her fate was. She'd decided the best choice was to be prepared for anything.

***

"Hurry up girl! Where is your trunk? And where is that coach?" Nyriee was in fine form today. Her strange mood had broken to reveal the thunderstorm always below. Something had been destroyed and Sereen had been screamed at several times already. Instead of fighting with Nyriee she went to grab her worn trunk. So far this was the first indication that Nyriee had given as to her plans for Sereen. It was making her tired just trying to figure it out. She almost wished Nyriee would just leave her at the house. What need did she have of her at court? She could as easily remain behind, it would be like taking a vacation. A vacation from Nyriee and her odious prodigy.

"Girls, come quickly the carriage is here!" Nyriee's shrill voice echoed throughout the entire house, sometimes Sereen swore she amplified it, no one with a voice like hers should be heard in the cellar.

The hard rap on the door was Sereen's cue to acknowledge their transport. She barely kept her mouth from gaping open when she found Slate dressed to the nines outside the door, dressed in the gaudiest clothing imaginable. He smiled benevolently at her, like one would a child below their notice. His gaze zeroed in on Nyriee and he pushed past her.

"Ma'am we're her to collect ye and yer things." Business first, in classic style, then the girl.

Nyriee nodded regally. "Of course, everything is here, our servant will help direct you."

So it went over the next hour that Sereen directed and helped load the carriage. Her feet were thoroughly soaked and she was shivering by the time they were done, but everything was on, checked and rechecked.

When Slate gave her a proprietary look Sereen found that she'd like nothing better than to hit him, which surprised her, normally she wasn't prone to violence. It shocked her even more when he walked over to Nyriee and instead of bowing his head he looked her straight in the eye and—

"Ma'am, I know ye don' know me. Ye see here, I'm the Innkeeper's son, set ta' inherit the whole gig when he passes on. So I'm set for life see. An' I'd like to ask ye if ye'd give me Sereen to be me bride. She's the only piece tha' be, ah, missin'. I've seen 'round enough to know she's a darned hard worker and would make me an exco-llent companion."

Nyriee looked down her nose at him, despite his height, as regal as any queen, pursed her thin lips and said, "No." With the finality of a book being snapped closed. Never had she been so glad for Nyriee's selfishness.

Slate looked like he'd just been shot in the stomach. His face screwed up and he looked scary, all of the creepiness she'd contemplated so long coming to the forefront. If she'd been given to him this was what she'd have had to contend with every single day, the threat of a whipping if she displeased him in any manner. It looked as if he'd like to do it right then, but because of Nyriee's station was unable to. She got the feeling he wasn't used to being denied in any manner, over anything.

It took him several minutes to compose himself, during which Nyriee looked at him as if he was a bug, imposing his presence upon her. "Why? She'll no be gettin' any be'er offers, such as she is."

Sereen felt tears sting her eyes at his cruel words. They were painfully true. She was plain and taller than was proper. Her red hair with its curl was a fight everyday to keep contained in its place. Her eyes were her best features, a dancing purple hue, everything else was too grey, too drab. Her eyes stood out like beacons on her face, the only part of her that didn't look like something seen through a murky pool. She lacked luster, was plain, boring. She was an ugly duckling and it was all too true that she was unlikely to receive a better offer than his.

Nyriee looked like she was swallowing that bug just speaking to him. It was painfully apparent to everyone that he was wasting *her* time and therefore he should be quiet and disappear like a good bug, one that wanted to survive.

When she spoke her words dripped with contempt. "This household is not yet ready to release her. And if it were it certainly wouldn't be to the likes of *you*."

He seemed to shrink before their eyes, his bravado withering away, he slunk away glowering at the carriage man, who only smiled a nasty smile.

They all piled into the carriage with Slate sitting up with the driver. The ride was very uncomfortable. It was smooth enough, all the carriages had runners instead of wheels, and were easily changed on and off for the three summer months. Allowing for a far easier trip.

She sat next to Floria, who wasn't as bad as the other two. She didn't want to move over much, afraid of drawing attention to herself. As it was it seemed the entire conversation had been forgotten, the girls chatted constantly about the Prince and their grand plans for when they arrived. How he'd fall instantly in love with one of them and they'd be married in a glorious wedding. No mention was made of his less savory pursuits.

The first stop of the carriage ride was dropping Slate off at the Inn. Surprisingly Nyriee also got off the carriage, following Slate into the Inn.

She returned with a satisfied smile on her face. In the distance Sereen could see Miriam, Slate, and the Innkeeper, their faces were clouded, and they were all talking animatedly, angrily. She had a feeling that she'd no longer be welcomed at the Inn.

They didn't stop again until the following night. Nyriee wanted to reach the court as quickly as possible, and they weren't very close to it. For a woman who wanted to be as powerful and recognized as Nyriee, it had never made since why she lived as far from court as was possible, without entering the Tundra. But many things about Nyriee were confounding and threw one off, like why she would take in an orphan for no reason when it seemed she was cruel and heartless. Sereen learned to take notice of the oddities and move on.

***

By the last day of their twelve day journey Sereen was ready to scream and was seriously thinking about Slate's proposal. At least if she'd accepted she wouldn't have had to ride in the carriage. Nyriee was in a witch of a mood, snapping at anyone that dared voice a complaint, it had silenced the whining of her daughters, who had subsided into a pouts, thinking to punish with silence.

Sereen had tried to sleep as much as possible, or feign it, finding it was the easiest way to avoid conversation and not get thrown into the middle of fights and insults. For some inexplicable reason she felt exceptionally worn out. Nyriee on the other hand looked lovelier than ever, travel appeared to suite her.

She'd been staring sightlessly out the window when Christmas Town came into view, the capital of Christmas Land. All paintings paled in comparison. Blanketed in icy snow it looked like a city of diamonds set against a blue canvas. It took her breath away, and gave it back to her. Smiling secretly to herself she glanced at everyone else out of the corner of her eye, to see Nyriee staring coldly at her. Her daughter leaned over in her lap, her hand resting on her hair.

"It's a beautiful sight, is it not?" Her voice was soft, and carried deadly shards of ice hidden within it.

Sereen nodded reluctantly, it felt insulting to the town to agree with her, but it was true. Nyriee's words were more akin to an insult, than a compliment to the town.

"It's been a long time since I've had the pleasure of seeing this vision of beauty. It is a grand honor, one you should relish in." Nyriee went back to stroking her daughter's hair and staring out the opposite window. Sereen felt dirtied by Nyriee's words, her joy diminished, until the carriage rounded a corner and she was swept away by the majesty of the town again. Not even Nyriee's sharp words to her daughters' to wake up intruded on the vision.

People dressed in brightly colored clothing strolled around the town, Elves, Elfin, a Fairy here and there, and animals of all shapes and sizes meandered their way around. The shops were all brightly lit, beckoning people in. It was festive and the nearer it got to Christmas the more decorated and celebratory it would get. In the mortal realm it was just a week away from Halloween, they weren't even thinking of

Christmas, it was still a distant thought. Here they acknowledged the other holidays and on Halloween there would be children trick-or-treating, but it was with the solid knowledge under it that it was all a diversion to take one's mind off Christmas. It was the first holiday to cross off the calendar marking the start of the franticness and beginning of the Christmas Countdown.

The carriage continued its glide up the slope to the Christmas Palace, glittering like a jewel on its hill. Snow wasn't yet packed on the street, here and there you could see patches of the cobblestone road below. A gentle snow was drifting down, helping to cover up those remaining blank spots. People spared glances towards the carriage, but she had a feeling carriages had been pouring in night and day, another one was no big deal.

It took a good two hours to make it through town to the Palace. As they drew closer they saw Ladies, dressed to splendid expense, taking a turn about the town. Areenie's shrill voice squawked insults and angrily exclaimed about how many there were.

"For sure we won't even have decent rooms, oh Mother! we shall end up no better than the lowest beggars! How shall we ever catch the Prince if we are poor cousins to these Ladies?"

Sereen rolled her eyes at Areenie's dramatics. They wouldn't get the rooms that they'd wanted, but she doubted they'd be treated like beggars. The Palace would have plenty of lavish rooms to place these three in and find a spare pallet for her to sleep upon.

As they reached the Palace proper she couldn't help but stare in wonder at it. When the carriage pulled to a stop the other three gestured for her to exit first, since she was the lowliest one present. A polite footman helped her out of the carriage then turned to the others, dismissing her. It stung. She could have been a great Lady... but for her plain looks and tattered dress.

With a sigh she turned to directing the men that were unloading. Despite her plainness and her worn appearance she commanded attention when she requested it. Deferring to her mistress she managed to determine where their trunks needed to be taken and had the entire ordeal dealt with in a simple and orderly fashion, something that rarely happened with the influx of women, earning her the gratitude of the men.

She had the men eating out of her hand when not only did she let them show their exceptional knowledge of the Palace, but she also thanked them profusely for their services. It was their job, but nonetheless it it was nice to know that someone appreciated what they did.

Once she got everything all settled in the suite, she sent out the clothing for washing and general clean up. Nyriee, upon arrival, had informed the girls that they would be going shopping the next day to find more suitable vestments. Sereen thought their dresses, with a minimal amount of effort, would have the same effect as something brand new, not that she would voice her opinion, it would only serve to get her a lashing.

That night she fell onto her pallet worn to the bone, but strangely content as well. Everything had gone very well so far, everyone was being very helpful and pleasant. She fell asleep with a content smile on her face, feeling, for some strange reason, more relaxed than she had for quite some time.

***

Prince Kristopher Kringle Claus, or Kris as he preferred, bent low over his horse, urging it faster. His friends had already fallen behind and still he pushed.

Faster. If he went fast enough he could outrun all of his troubles, all the disappointments, everything.

The speed was exhilarating. Everything was a blur of white. He could see the end of the cleared area coming up, beyond it pure white snow, never touched. He sat up slowly allowing the horse to slow down gradually, pulling it to a complete stop just before it was about to hit the bank. Despite the knowledge he should turn around and head back, that the horse needed a cool down walk, he sat there staring out over the pure expanse. What would it take to simply disappear into it and never have to worry about anything?

Today he was supposed to start heading home, back to his father and the evidence of what a disappointment he'd been throughout his entire life. The proof was irrefutable, no matter how much he wanted to deny it. His wandering ways had finally come home to roost with his father's pronouncement that he needed to pick a bride.

It would be easy to disappear into the snow and never worry about his father. He wished he could, his friends all thought he was crazy for not putting up a fight to rival all fights over this, but truth be told he was tired of seeing that resigned, disappointed look in his father's eyes every time he looked at him. Which was probably why he didn't go home very often.

Nudging his horse around he looked at his friends, already started back towards the warmth of the Inn and contemplated his insanity at agreeing to this. He could control his wild ways, he could stop, except it was such a strong lure, what was one more disappointment? One more reason why he didn't go home?

No, it was time. Time to face the music and settle down so that his father would no longer look at him and wonder how much longer his son would be on the Naughty List.

Chapter Two

Nyriee was in a devil of a mood and Sereen was ready to disappear. The dresses she'd bought for her daughters' weren't completely perfect, so she'd assigned Sereen to fix them up properly, except she couldn't decide what perfect was. With one ear to Palace gossip and another turned to her own preferences she kept wavering back and forth. It was driving Sereen mad and making Nyriee crabbier than ever. Already several times today she'd thought fondly of wrapping her hands around Nyriee's throat and shaking her until her brain set back together properly and all of the baloney she'd been dealing with lately was gone.

She took a step back from the dress she'd been working on and contemplated it. From what she'd heard from the maids, who would know, he liked low cut dresses with a tight fit. His favorite color was a blue almost as pale as the snow itself. None these dresses were going to fulfill that requirement, as they were a festive green, but it was something useful to know.

Moving to the Palace meant she no longer had to complete menial tasks, but instead had more odious ones, the more difficult the better it seemed. Like these dresses. She snuck a glance at the clock, they'd gone down to dinner half an hour ago, hoping to catch sight of the Prince. Rumor had it he was due to return at any time from his latest expedition, and everyone wanted to be the first he saw.

Shaking her head she turned away from the dress. He wasn't going to remember anyone, his only hope was if he had an exceptional memory, otherwise he'd never remember so much as a name with all of the Ladies present. It wouldn't matter if you were first, or last.

The Ladies had been pouring into the Palace. She wagered it was filled nearly to capacity. Whenever she went down to the kitchens the word was that they had summoned in more help to keep up with everything. Ladies were everywhere and it was difficult to find a moment of quiet in the mass of life. But with the commencement of the wife hunt in just two days time it made a kind of macabre sense. Everyone was hoping to be The-One-the-Prince-Chose. The dress shops were overloaded with orders and were selling fabric and dresses as quickly as the orders came in. Everything was overloaded and overbooked. Many of those in court had never been before and they wanted to see everything.

At first Sereen had thought it might calm down as the weeks lengthened, but had quickly decided that with the numbers it wasn't going to happen, that and it was becoming the most fanatic season of the year. It would only get more ridiculous and insane the deeper into the season it went.

That was why here she was working on dresses while everyone else was out being wined and dined into oblivion. It was quiet though, a quiet that would be shattered the moment she stepped out the door. She'd finally come up with a way to make the dress *perfect*, a way that could get her beaten, but was better than the current situation where she was constantly working on it and under constant threat of being beaten.

Having never met the Prince, or even seen him for that matter, it was difficult to determine precisely what would appeal to him. For Nyriee and the girls it was easy to know, but she was working in the dark with the Prince, hopefully she got lucky.

Carefully taking the key off the hook she locked the door and started towards the sewing room, on the hunt for something to touch off the dress perfectly. The dress that was giving her fits was Areenie's. Since she was quite obviously the most likely to catch the Prince's eye in a positive way, she also needed to be the most perfect. Extra care and attention went into this dress.

She had conflicting feelings about whether or not she wanted the Prince to fall in love with one of the girls, so she'd decided to stand in the middle, impartial, and watch what were guaranteed to be spectacular fireworks.

Moving with the silence of a specter down the halls she looked like one as well. Since arriving at the palace she'd felt much improved, but still looked like a ghost raised from the grave. Thankfully no one was about as she moved quickly along. She didn't want run into anyone and be mistaken for a maid and sent on an errand for one of the all too mighty.

Somehow she managed to make it to the seamstress's room without mishap. The woman, Madame Lacrofft had precisely what she wanted and Sereen thanked her profusely. The woman was just as thrilled to have helped out, because it meant just as much to her that there was one less dress she had to work on and one less disgruntled Lady throwing a fit when it didn't meet her exacting specifications.

After her success she decided to make her way towards the kitchens. She didn't get to eat unless she managed to scrounge her own food and the longer after dinner one went the less likely it was for one to come away with a meal.

Lately she'd been feeling horrible, like something was draining her. She'd made sure she was eating, but it didn't matter, since coming to the Palace she'd lost weight and looked more horrid than ever. One of the reasons Nyriee was so snappish was that she wasn't doing so well either, she'd been looking older lately, like the world was wearing on her.

She turned down the wrong hallway and had gone a little ways before she realized it.

Soft noises echoed up and down the hall and she came to a stunned halt when she realized that a couple was kissing. She was horrified that she'd come upon such behavior.

Some sound must have issued out of her shocked self, because the man turned towards her, and *winked*! The act spurred her to action, she turned and fled down the hall, his deep laughter rolling through the hall after her. Her cheeks flaming the entire way, hoping to forget the entire thing.

Kris bent and picked up the fabric the appalled servant had dropped, brushing it off. The maid, Allisone, he'd been kissing had run off immediately after she'd realized what had distracted him. She'd been mortified at getting caught, no more than the girl that'd happened upon them though.

With a laugh he turned away and started after her, heading toward Madame Lacrofft, hopefully the kindly woman would remember her. He shuddered at the idea of the girl working for the seamstress, if she told her, and it got back to his father…shudder. Hopefully he could find her before she told anyone. Maybe coax her into keeping the sordid tale a secret. He didn't want his father having further proof of his misconduct. Allisone had completely ruined his plans to behave himself. Almost the moment he'd stepped in the door she'd grabbed him. He hoped she was happy with the trouble she'd caused.

***

After fumbling for several minutes to unlock the door with badly shaking hands, Sereen had finally managed and had promptly slammed it shut, locking it the moment she was inside. Out of breath and panicky she leaned against the door, trying to regain her faculties, and realized that somewhere along her mad dash she'd dropped the fabric. She pressed the butt of her hand to her forehead, groaning.

Now the dress wouldn't be finished by the time they got back and she'd have to go explain to the seamstress about the fabric. Or maybe she could go retrieve it, and get something to eat she remembered as her stomach growled. But not yet. She'd wait until she was sure the couple was gone, it wouldn't do for her to run into them again. With a sigh she got herself something to drink, her thoughts drifting back to the man.

He'd been handsome, even in the dim lighting he'd been striking with his dark hair, having some quality beyond his looks as well, something that commanded attention. He'd been tall, taller than her by several inches at least. She bet he made all of the Ladies in the castle feel petite.

Wishing she'd seen his face better she turned towards general tidying up. The chances of running into him again were slim she was sure, and even if she did she didn't know if she'd be able to identify him. He'd had a presence though, something that had drawn her, it would be hard to miss. Giving a small laugh she shook her head, men like that stood out no matter what the situation or setting, they imposed and impressed.

Sereen jumped when she heard the firm knocks on the door. She stared at it for several seconds, contemplating it as if it was a particularly poisonous snake. More of the knocks and she was moving across the floor, tugging the door open before she pondered her witless actions.

It was him! She gaped up at him, shocked he'd had the audacity to follow her. Before she got a word out he barged into the suite, forcing her to step back. Up close she barely came up to his chest, he was large and imposing. He was dressed in worn garments that looked like a servant's. She started backing away and didn't stop until his hand reached out and wrapped around her arm. It was rare for men to be taller than her, even Slate was barely at eye level, but this man made her feel short. A feeling she'd never had the pleasure of feeling. She kept moving side to side, trying to escape.

"Hey, stop dancing around. I'm not here to hurt you," His voice was perfect, husky and deep. It was immediately clear why the maid had done something as crazy as stand in the hall kissing him, his voice would have been lure enough. "I just came to bring you this." He held out the fabric she'd dropped.

"Oh! Thank you." Subdued she reached for it, and he pulled it just out of reach, holding it above her grasp.

"What are you doing?" Glaring at him she tried for the fabric again, only to have it moved further out of reach. Subsiding she gave him a dark look. "Are you planning on holding it hostage and annoying me to death?" Casting a quick glance towards the fabric she turned her eyes back to him. "I need that fabric for milady's dress, I'll be in no end of trouble. Give it to me."

The cad had the nerve to grin at her. She was taken aback again by how handsome he was, he reminded her of royalty with his devilish good looks and his overwhelming presence. "Hmm, I think I need some kind of repayment for my services, and your earlier interruption."

Her cheeks flushed scarlet. "Ooh, how dare you mention that! You should be paying me, why I should report you to-to someone! Kissing in halls like—like some nobleman! Give me my fabric!"

It wasn't considered proper for a servant to be kissing in the halls, briefly she considered the possibility he was a nobleman, but dismissed it. A nobleman wouldn't have brought her the fabric.

For several moments he was silent, contemplating her. Then a mischievous grin lit up his face. "Well now, I suppose I could let it go for a kiss, since mine was interrupted. Come on sweetheart, give us a kiss."

It was her turn to be flabbergasted, "You want a kiss? From me?" Her voice squeaked on her last words and her cheeks were flushed scarlet red, making her look the most alive she had in years. "You know what, fine.

Anything to get rid of you." Without giving it a moment's consideration she rolled up on her toes and pressed her lips to his, and just as quickly rocked back. That task done she returned to glaring at him. She wanted him to leave so she could get back to work, and give her the fabric. Frantically she ignored the zing of the kiss. It was one of the most daring things she'd done in her life and didn't want to think of it.

He gave her funny look and reluctantly released her, handing her the fabric, obviously unsatisfied with the kiss, but unable to renege on the deal. He gave a mock salute and started to leave, on his way out the door he turned back and gave her a saucy wink, and speaking in low tones he said, "I hope you don't think that's a real kiss."

And was gone.

She hurried into the hall, watching until he disappeared around the bend. Touching gentle fingers to her lips she marveled at the electricity in that simple kiss. Her gaze caught on the dress and she plopped down, wishing she knew more about the mystery man. She'd just kissed someone for the first time and she didn't even know his name! Or even the color of his eyes. In the dim light with the candles at his back they'd been remained in shadows.

Feeling more alive and energized than she had in years she reached for the dress and sat down. Ready to start working.

***

Kris slammed his door shut, breathless and laughing, at himself. He was such an idiot. He couldn't believe he'd challenged the girl to kiss him. Sereen. It had been folly too. The shock of that kiss still held him. He'd never felt such power from such a simple kiss and from such a plain thing to. At least at first she'd looked plain, after the kiss she'd looked so alive, so vibrant, before he would have thought her a walking corpse.

The kiss itself, a bare brush of lips, shouldn't have been so electric, but lo and behold the chaste kiss had packed a more powerful punch than any ale he'd ever drunk.

Shaking his head he tried to put her out of his head. She had no idea who he was and she'd probably fall over dead if she found out.

She seemed to be a proper little thing, though she hadn't acted too proper, just kissing him. Probably the most impulsive thing she'd ever done in her life. His goal in life, to make boring lives like hers more interesting.

When he'd gone to see Madame Lacrofft she'd informed him that she was a servant to the Lady Dantaan. She hadn't been able to disguise her shock at his inquiry.

"Seems to be a little below your notice, don't it your highness?" Her knowing look had rankled, despite its truth. As a rule he tended to go after the beautiful creatures of the court, she wasn't even pretty, though there had been something…something with those vibrant purple eyes, they'd looked alive, and out of place on that face. Like all the rest of her could fade, but those eyes would endure.

With a groan he vaulted off his bed. He needed to change out of these clothes before someone else mistook him for a servant. They were filthy from the road and well worn.

It wouldn't do him any good to think about her or anyone else right now, he needed to figure out how to evade his father's matchmaking scheme. Oddly enough though he couldn't put the girl out of his mind, it continuously strayed back to her, going in a constant loop. Don't think about her, think about her, how to escape matchmaking, think about her, don't think about her, that kiss was tantalizing, don't think of her, any other maids to kiss? Back to her again. An endless circle in his head.

    According to Madame Lacrofft Sereen's mistress was a royal witch, and she'd been thankful to get rid of the woman. More than thankful, ecstatic. She'd shaken her head about Sereen, saying that she seemed to be the sweetest thing. How someone with such a kind nature had stayed such being tormented by the cruel Nyriee was beyond her. And cruel she was. She'd said that none of the servants spoke a single good word of her, worse than the most horrendous courtier, she was mean hearted and spiteful.

    Madame Lacrofft had informed him Sereen was well liked though, despite her somewhat less than appealing looks. She was respected and almost everyone was fond of her. Even with him she'd been good-natured, and there was something about her, something compelling, that made you pay her mind.

    He wanted to see her again, to learn how she'd remained so sweet with such an evil mistress. To understand how such vibrant eyes could live in such a sallow face.

    Ugh, he put his arm over his eyes, laying back on his bed, she didn't even know who he was. How would she react if she learned he was the Prince? She'd probably be the most polite and civilized creature in Christmas Land, like everyone else, instead of the spitfire that had threatened him. Cursing he turned off his light. Sometimes he hated being the Prince.

***

The dress was stunning, it's model, not so much. It was a shame that its splendor was wasted on Areenie. Though the dress did add something to her, no dress could overcome the defects of its owner.

Areenie flaunted much Floria's consternation. Only one daughter was having all the money and lavish attention, because only one of them had a chance. Sereen felt bad for Floria as their mother cast all her attentions on her elder sister.

She'd heard that other men, also looking for wives, had come to court hoping to catch a beautiful Lady who couldn't catch the much wanted attentions of a Prince. If she was a Lady she'd drop the notion of trying to snag the Prince and go after one of the powerful Lords, who would be feeling lonely without their normal attentions.

With a twirl Areenie halted in front of her mother. "Oh mother the dress is beautiful, quite perfect to catch the eye of the Prince."

Maternal pride glittered in Nyriee's eyes. "The first step my dear. You shan't have to wait much longer to be on his arm. It's a wonder we haven't seen him yet." There was a snide undertone to the words. She like, so many other mamas, thought it was exceptionally rude that the Prince had yet to grace them with his much desired presence. The servants had stated spitefully that if they were the Prince they'd go into hiding as well, none of them were pleased by the invasion of women in their court. They took great pride in their work and were insulted daily by these new comers who thought they knew all.

Several pirouettes later Areenie and Floria disappeared back into their rooms and Nyriee turned to her, with a cold smile on her face.

"Good job, girl, finally we've found a good use for you." Her tone and words were a slap in the face. Impotent anger filled Sereen with no release. As far as she'd determined beatings and whippings weren't permitted in the courts, but there were other punishments...And Sereen would rather not have to deal with any form of punishment.

"We have other dresses coming in, they shall be placed in your capable hands."

It should have been a glowing compliment, that Nyriee thought her good enough to work on the dresses, but instead it was degrading, dredging up Slate's words. What if they all were right? That she'd never be better than this? Tears welled in her eyes. She held them in with a steely grip. Barely.

Dressing them all seemed to take hours and through it all she felt drained and broken, ready to collapse at any moment.

The moment they were gone she collapsed on her pallet, scalding tears pouring down her cheeks. Every time she tried to stop some other memory would intrude, causing a fresh torrent.

A hand pressed against her shoulder gently. She jumped, almost out of her skin.

"Hey sweetheart, calm down I don't bite."

His voice washed over her with a calming effect. It reminded her of warm chocolate, deep and smooth. Instead of continuing to try to escape she turned and pressed herself deep into his hold and sobbed. He held her as she cried, gentling her. Slowly with hiccupping breaths the tears abated. He continued to stroke his hand along her back, soothing.

She couldn't remember the last time she'd been held, been comforted, and she'd missed it, more than she'd imagined. If it weren't for the animals she'd probably have gone mad from lack of contact. She wasn't of those robot things the humans had.

"Are you alright?" His tone was gentle, finishing the job of quieting her.

Nodding, she clung tighter to him, savoring the warmth and contact. Instead of shoving away an obviously clinging female he squeezed her tighter. It was with a sigh she realized that no matter how comfortable she felt she was keeping him from something else. Resigned she moved quickly to stand, catching his chin with her head.

"Oh, I'm so sorry!" Reaching out she rubbed her fingers across his jaw. Gently, he grasped her fingers in his hand.

"It's alright, don't worry about it. Is your head okay?"

"Yes." And the way he was rubbing her fingers was highly distracting. Pulling their fingers to his chin he pressed her fingers to his face. "I'm alrigh—" His eyes widened and he looked around, jerking her from trying to figure out the color of his eyes.

"What time is it?" He glanced around frantically. Taking a quick glance at the clock right behind his head she told him. Vaulting to his feet he took off towards the door, disappearing without a backwards glance.

Bewildered she sat there for several minutes, before shaking herself and standing. Confusion warred with anger for a moment before she got it under wraps. Why did he keep showing up and running off?

***

The servants had told her she could watch the festivities with them, the commencement of the bride hunt. They'd even snuck her a gown so she'd blend in, so she wouldn't get in trouble. The way she understood it they rotated throughout the evening so everyone would get a chance to watch at least some of the happenings. It was a tradition, a way of allowing everyone to enjoy the evening.

It was the most organized chaos she'd ever seen. People, rushing back and forth, servants primping, everyone moving as fast as they could. They all recognized her and quickly shuffled her into the capable hands of the watchers.

When the Palace had been built it had been planned in such a manner that everyone could enjoy the merriment of Christmas Hall, including the servants. There were discreet balconies raised above the crowd's heads and tiered artfully to increase the grandeur of the hall rather than detract. Its architect had been brilliant, catering to every need, leaving none out.

In short time she found herself on one such balcony barely above the vast sea of heads gazing at the splendor before her.

As yet there were no true Christmas decorations up, but the hall had been wrought with it in mind. A Nativity was set above the heads of the audience and the flow pattern of the floor revealed a rise in its center were a giant Christmas tree would stand, with niches in the floor to help anchor its stand. The hall's roof rose high to allow for the largest Christmas tree possible and all along the walls were places for wreathes and garland.

Along the high ceiling were Christmas lights, not yet turned on. The walls had Christmas images carved into them and almost seemed to move and dance.

Below a swarm of butterflies now ruled in their gracious beauty. Everywhere one looked there were swarms of brilliantly colored dresses glimmering and glistening in the magic light. On a raised dais against the wall adjacent to her balcony rested three chairs. The one in the middle was its largest and the one on the left bore a bouquet of vibrant purple flowers, ethereal in their beauty.

The hall was open during all hours of the day, but she'd not had the courage or time to see it. Supposedly if you wanted you could even sit on the King's high seat. None of the royal party was currently visible.

Since his wife's death, some one-hundred and twenty odd years ago, the King had become more and more of a recluse. The people rarely saw jolly old Saint Nick any more. He'd become more of a figurehead than a real person, similar to how he was viewed in the mortal realm.

Several shifts came and went as the butterflies danced. She passed the time chatting with the other girls about dresses, which ones were their personal favorites and so on. There was a lot of blue floating around the dance floor, many made snide comments about it, discussing the fact the Prince was just as likely to fall for someone wearing a brown bag as he was his favorite color, they'd at least stand out. Sereen understood their unspoken words as well. She wasn't sure how many servants the Prince had pursued, but she'd wager it was a great deal. It seemed that all of them were endeared with him, and in honesty who could blame them?

None of them really thought the Prince would marry by Christmas. He was smart and would find a loop hole, if there were any he was wily enough to dig it up. Others said he'd marry alright, but not for love, wink, wink. It was painfully obvious that none of them were enthused about the arrangement. But all of them, unanimously it seemed, loved the idea of him marrying, even out of their clutches, if it meant he was in love with the girl. Not forced to marry her.

Slowly all the dancers stopped and she could see them moving apart, the motion rippling across the dancers until there was a path, directly to the thrones.

Santa walked regally down the swath. Even from the distance Santa looked worn, tired. In his many years time had stooped him. His beard looking more grey than white, looking old against his red suit.

If anyone around her noticed, they didn't comment. They either hadn't observed it because the change had been gradual or they didn't wish to speak of it. She wanted to send him back to his room and do something to make him feel better. Undoubtedly his son wasn't helping matters. Thinking about it, she figured that Kristopher must be somewhere around one-hundred and fifty years old, old enough to behave himself. But instead of taking some of the responsibility and workload of his father's shoulder he was up to no good.

She'd never had such an opportunity, at a mere nineteen she was a babe to most of the people here, many of them over fifty years old. The Elfin were gifted with longevity of life, most living over a thousand years.

When Santa sat down the dancing began again. He glanced periodically at the seat to the right of his. Obviously his son was acting a no show. The servants were whispering among themselves about the happenings of the dance when she noticed a man sneaking into the hall from a side door.

He was dressed richly from his head to his toes. He bore a marked resemblance to the man she'd caught. She'd decided to not tell on him, she'd wager the maids loved him and they wouldn't appreciate him getting in trouble. It wasn't like he'd been doing anything nasty, he'd just been kissing someone.

The man made a beeline straight for Santa. People parted for him, moving quickly out of the way. Upon reaching the dais he whispered in Santa's ear. A joyful smile split the old Elf's face, bringing one to her own. She wondered who he was that could make Santa smile so happily.

Santa motioned one of the Elves over and told them something, they nodded, and scurried off.

She couldn't shake the feeling that she'd seen the man before. He seemed familiar. Rubbing her eyes she turned away for several minutes. Taking a quick glance at the clock that hung on the wall opposite the deck she stood on, she found it was very close to midnight. Midnight was supposed to signify the beginning of the bride hunt, but so far, besides the excited chatter of those below, she could find no indication of its commencement.

At five minutes to midnight Santa stood. His deep voice rolled through Christmas Hall, garnering everyone's undivided attention. The man continued to stand, his back to her.

"Ladies and gentlemen of all Christmas Land. Welcome!" No matter how tired he may be in appearance his voice reflected all the best of the holiday season.

"We all know why you've come, many different reasons all, but at the core, the same." He took a glance back to the man, still facing away. "Weeks ago I bid all the marriageable Ladies of the land to the Christmas Court, so that my son could pick a wife from among them. Or perhaps hurry his way towards one outside these walls. So," He paused, taking a look around the entire hall, including her and the servants standing on all the platforms. His gaze seemed to touch and probe everyone, particularly all of those speaking in hushed tones about those outside these walls. "With great pleasure I present my son, and the bride hunt is on!"

There was thunderous cheering from the crowd as St. Nicholas finished his speech and his son, the man next to him, turned towards the awaiting assembly. He stood staring out over the crowd, much as his father had done, his gaze sweeping over everyone, and when he looked up at the platform, her mouth dropped open in shock.

***

Kris was sprinting down the hall, as fast as his legs could carry him. He'd forgotten all about the meeting with his father and was going to be very late. He hazarded a glance down at his shirt and breathed a sigh of relief when he noticed it wasn't stained. Not that he'd have been angry. She'd needed a shoulder, and he was glad he'd been able to offer some companionship to her. No one should cry alone. With a groan he realized that he had no idea why she'd been crying like her world had ended.

Hopefully it wasn't anything so dire. He wasn't sure what had possessed him to go see her, something about that kiss he supposed, and to find her alone in tears had torn at something visceral. His only thought had been to comfort her. A creature that life had dumped a stinking heap on.

Racing around a corner he almost collided with two servants kissing. They jumped apart with a startled scream and he yelled, "Sorry!" over his shoulder as he continued his sprint.

Skidding to a stop he straightened his shirt and worked to calm his breathing as the hallway bent in the final corner before his father's room. His father would still know he'd been running, but he'd look somewhat decent.

Smoothing back his unruly hair he went in. His father was sitting at his desk writing away on The List. There were two Lists: The Naughty and Nice List, and the Presents List. Every year they got bombarded with scads of letters, some containing lists others, not. Not everything on those lists was what people wanted and some things people simply forgot, all of this had to be sorted through so everyone had the best chance of getting what they wanted. Truth be told he'd always been afraid of what he'd find if he helped with The List, that he'd been a disappointment, that he was on the Naughty List.

"Hold on a moment."

Kris felt like tapping his foot, but refrained. He'd made his father wait, so he in turn would practice patience. Tired lines framed his father's face, his beard more grey than white and silver. He tried to remember when it had happened but realized with a shock he didn't know, the best he could think was it had happened around the time his mother had died.

It was rare for Elves to die, his mom hadn't been one as his father was, but as Queen of Christmas Land she'd been an immortal. Just as his bride would be. Her death had come as a shocking blow, she'd been in excellent health with no signs of aught being wrong.

Early on, and shamefully even now, he'd tested the limits of his strength, his ability to remain among the living despite the suicidal things he attempted. He supposed that was one of the reasons he'd not been around his father of late. His father thought that you should respect your immortality, acknowledge its gift, but not go out and test, to push its limits. He knew his father was right, but he still rebelled. Santa Claus was right, he was perfect, beyond reproach. And it rankled. Why did he have to always be right about everything? Couldn't he be wrong now and again?

Standing now Santa moved around the room with a grace that belied his girth. For someone as large as Santa he was one of the healthiest and most fit people in Christmas Land. Though Kris had to admit that lately his father's sparkling blue eyes had been muted, tired, like the world was weighing down on him.

Giving him an askance glance Santa offered Kris some cocoa. Once that minor task was completed, Santa settled himself back into his chair and raked Kris with a knowing look.

"I see that you were waylaid," He gestured towards Kris's shirt, and automatically Kris looked down. The shirt was almost dry, but you could tell here and there that it had been damp. "Slip and fall, no, you'd be all wet, hmm. Did you break another poor girl's heart?" His father's dry voice, was serious, and he was reminded again of his earlier thoughts. Had he really been so bad that his father now believed that everything he did was related to heartbreaking?

"I was comforting her. I'm unsure what was wrong."

"Hmm, I see. Kris, you are aware—" With a deep sigh he stopped and stared at his drink, seeming lost for a moment. "Kris, I want you to pick the best woman, she doesn't have to be one of these Ladies. Pick the one that you can imagine spending the rest of your life with, choose for—"

A gentle tap, tap on the door had both of their heads turning. It was one of the Elves, come to tell them Santa was needed in workshop. Kris thought about excusing himself, but at his father's knowing look he decided to go with him instead, to prove him wrong.

The workshop issues took longer than they should of, and during them Kris got his clothes completely covered in all kind of things and had to change them, which ruined his plans of walking into Christmas Hall with his father. It wasn't the end of his world by any means, but still…

As he walked with measured steps towards the hall he had to admit his main desire was to turn right back around and flee the other direction as fast as possible. For the last month, since the first summons had gone out, he'd been avoiding the hall, avoiding all of this.

When it wasn't being used for a ball it had tables in it, where everyone came and went eating or just visiting. There was a great fireplace on one end of the hall where chairs were set out no matter the time, to sit relax, and just stare into the flames. He wished he knew why he'd agreed to this, normally he ignored the edicts of his father, but this time for some reason beyond his ken he'd acquiesced to his request. So here he was, going to brave a horde of marriage hungry Ladies and their mothers.

With one last tug on his shirt he slipped into the hall. Some of the crowd recognized him and moved out of his way, everyone else followed their lead and he moved quickly through the milling crowd. No one was dancing, instead standing around waiting for him, probably. He spoke quickly to his father, informing him he was ready to get this over with then waited while his father made his speech. He kept his face carefully turned away from the crowd, so no one could see his expression. It was difficult to control his expression with the tumult of emotions racing through him.

At his father's final words, he turned towards the crowd, looking out over the avid faces and suddenly had to look anywhere but at the false people before him, their only desire to grab him, and what he represented. He would wager that if asked about why they wanted to marry him it centered around his power, money, and maybe even his looks. Not to help others out, not out of love. Complete disgust and disenchantment flooded him, all he wanted was out.

To keep his eyes from the floor he looked towards the balconies, his eye catching on one of the balconies and the faces of the servants, a wide array of expressions reflected on their features. Unsure as to what he was searching for he continued to look until his eyes lit upon her. The moment he met her purple eyes they widened and a shocked expression filled her face. Suddenly he wished she didn't know. Amid all these false people dressed in all this finery she must view him as no better than them. His reputation coming to the fore and like never before he wished the actions of the past away, wished the honest creature above had no clue.

***

As soon as Sereen realized she was staring right into the Prince of Christmas Land's eyes she turned away, appalled by her behavior. She'd interrupted the Prince! She wanted to escape to get away as quickly as she could and go hide in some deep hole. Somehow she figured that nowhere was too far in regards to the Prince.

Instead of running off immediately, lest someone become suspicious she remained where she was, turning to the person beside her and striking a conversation. It was difficult to remain still while she didn't know if he was still watching her. The girl she was talking to was an excellent distraction, providing keen insight into the world below her.

When it became entirely unbearable she finally looked to where the Prince had stood on the dais. He wasn't there anymore and she felt both annoyed and relieved. She couldn't stop herself from peering into the crowd, looking for him. Despite her best attempts she couldn't locate him among the crowd, finally she gave up. Tired from the entire ordeal she took her leave.

Upon arriving at the rooms she changed and climbed into bed, hoping to sleep until Nyriee and her daughters returned. After tossing and turning, stuck in an endless loop of embarrassment and thoughts she went to sleep. Only to reawaken moments later it felt like to Nyriee's insistent, shrill voice in her ear.

The exhaustion of finding out who he was had worn her and made her fingers clumsy and in turn made Nyriee furious.

Nyriee was in a good enough mood about the ball and the occurrences therein that she didn't resort to blows, instead settling for a glower and glare in her direction.

***

For the next several days she laid low, avoiding everyone, and hiding out in her rooms. The only real problems came from the dresses, and Nyriee. Sereen couldn't shake the feeling that despite the fact that nothing had happened, that no one should have guessed, that Nyriee knew somehow. She watched her with a dark look on her face and rarely left her alone. It was hampering, but Sereen was in full hiding mode, so Nyriee's strange behavior helped.

After a week of being cooped up with Nyriee and her children however, Sereen was about to go crazy. Nyriee's strange behavior had not abated, rather it had grown worse and Areenie and Floria were constantly complaining, giving her a nasty headache.

They complained about anything and everything concerning the Prince, his absences most notably. It seemed that after the commencement ball he'd been only the most rare attendee. On those rare occasions he was present they gushed endlessly about his looks, what he wore, and who he deigned to speak to. The outfits the other Ladies wore were cut to ribbons in the safety of the suite.

No one was safe from their tongues. When the Prince danced, talked, or sat next to someone his every action was reviewed. It was obvious that he paid little mind to Floria and Areenie, though he was polite when they foisted themselves on him. No one creature had been set upon by the Prince's attentions yet, which made Floria and Areenie very pleased.

The dresses that she'd been assigned were completed in record time and before long all she had to do was help them dress, otherwise she read whatever books the maids would bring her, or she simply learned the gossip. If the servants thought it was strange that she'd gone into hiding they spoke nothing of it, though one of them did make a slight slip referring to Nyriee. They simply assumed she'd gotten in trouble by Nyriee.

Finally one evening while another ball was going on she slipped out of the room to go to the gardens. It should be safe now, he should have forgotten.

The gardens were magnificent, a truly stunning creation. Winter roses were everywhere, there would be a gorgeous bloom for Christmas. Everywhere were winter plants, intermingled with summer plants that could survive the winter. The path was a maze to the fountain in the center. Here and there were statues of all manner of things and hidden in the shadows of lattice works covered in vines were benches. A loving hand had crafted the garden with romance in mind.

It was on one of those hidden benches that Sereen chose to perch. Hidden there she could watch as the sun set low on the horizon and the ball goers came and went. It was amusing to watch how the upper crust acted while out in the snow, some so careful with their finery, while others romped in the snow.

The moon shone with a bright silvery light down onto the garden, finishing the job the lattices had started, wreathing her in complete shadow. No one noticed her as they took in the beauty of the garden. It was nice, the anonymity. There was a certain peace in it that couldn't be grasped any other way. Nyriee came into the garden, followed by a young Lord, and wandered about while he spoke nothings in her ear.

Sereen couldn't help but shake her head and barely kept from laughing as they went past. It was hard to imagine what the Lord thought he'd get out of Nyriee, though perhaps he thought to marry her for money. She looked like someone that should have money and power, enough to lure anyone, while in truth she had little.

Though as of late she'd looked more tired than usual, older. As if something was draining her. Despite Nyriee's cruelty she didn't want anything to happen to her, she'd taken her in after all.

After a while they both disappeared, but other couples came and went. She was certain she fell asleep for a while, for when she awoke the garden was empty. There was no risk of freezing to death, the areas around and the benches themselves were heated. It was a good thing too, since her cloak was threadbare, hardly fit for anything less than the rage pile. The warmth allowed other flowering plants that would normally be unable to blossom and flourish during the winter to do so as well.

A hushed peace had descended and despite the sure knowledge she'd get a beating for not being in the rooms she remained where she was, smiling as a soft snow started to sift onto the ground. It was a scene out of a dream, one of the happy, pleasant, ones.

Only marred by a man in a cloak creeping about. Here and there were a few lamps casting dim light, adding to that of the moon. If she hadn't been staring sightlessly at the edge of the light she'd never have seen him. He moved without a sound, leaving no trace behind him. He moved with unhurried steps towards the edge of the garden, only to stop and look back, searching the garden. It was a strange feeling, having someone look directly at you and not knowing if they could see you. She wasn't afraid he could see her, though a little thrill went through her when he stared at her spot for several seconds longer than needed, but finally he turned away and went back to creeping off to wherever he'd been going before.

As he disappeared she let out a pent up breath that she hadn't realized she'd been holding. Then laughed at her own silliness. It was probably some servant sneaking back from a night on the town, afraid of getting caught.

With a sigh she stood up, it was time for her to sneak back to her bed, or maybe spend the night in the kitchen. Either way it was time for bed. There had been peace out here, a peace that she found was becoming more and more reluctant to surrender.

The hand that clamped on her shoulder made her let out a startled scream and struggle to get away from the strong hands that held her shoulders.

"Hey, careful now, I don't bite." His grip tightened fractionally on her and finally she forced her self to go still, fighting would only make him more alert and if she wanted to escape she needed him unconcerned.

"Please release me, I haven't done *anything*." Logic was always the best course first, then she'd go to fighting. It had worked against Slate. Hopefully it would yield the same results here. She wished she could have kept her voice from warbling slightly at the end, letting the fear shine through.

"Of course you have, everyone's done something." His voice was smooth and gentle, reminding her of someone…

"Not to you, I'm sure, please let me go." For whatever strange reason the terror from moments ago was fading away at the sound of his voice. He must have cast a spell on her! Frantic now to escape this Wizard before he used her for some heinous crime, she struggled and pulled, finally breaking free. She scrambled over the powdery snow, unable to find a good purchase on the slick stuff.

"Oomph." One moment she was running as quickly as she was able and the next she was face down on a snow bank. She tried kicking and hitting, anything to escape, but nothing worked. Finally she was facing her attacker, arms and legs pinned to her sides, nothing to do except lay there while her attacker did his worst to her.

"I might not bite, but you do. What's got you all worked up?" The flight and fight had thrown back whatever hood he'd been wearing and his face was now partially revealed, though his eyes remained in shadows. It was the Prince!

Sereen groaned out loud when she realized who it was. It seemed she could do nothing right when it came to him. First interrupting him in the hall, then kissing him and being abrasive, now this, he'd have her sent to the Tundra for sure.

"Are you okay? I didn't mean to hurt you." His grip on her immediately loosened, but she didn't move, completely overcome by horror at her actions. Maybe she'd be given some decent clothing to wear; they wouldn't want her to freeze to death, would they?

"No, I'm fine, that is you didn't hurt me." Gahh, she wished he'd leave, so she could be alone and contemplate the stupidity of her actions.

"Sorry about that." He stood, though he kept a light hold on her cloak, as if afraid she might try to run away again. He helped her brush off her clothes, the snow had already melted and soaked her in several spots, but she ignored them, not wanting to reveal how poorly her mistress cared for her.

"It's okay."

"What were you doing out here?" There was unchecked speculation in his voice. "A romantic meeting? A plot?"

She shook her head, a flush spreading through her cheeks. "Of course not," Was he blind? No man would give her a second look, plain and boring didn't garner attention. That was probably what he was up to. "What were you doing out here, sneaking around?"

"Ahh, you see I snuck off to avoid the matchmaking mamas at the ball and have a bit of fun. Normally this is completely deserted at this time, an excellent route back to my rooms, but not tonight. What are you doing here, hiding in the shadows?" He didn't even have the temerity to look embarrassed that he'd been avoiding the ball, rather he looked dashing and gallant, the very image of the bad boy Prince.

"I wasn't hiding, I was enjoying the night and suddenly a prowler attacks me!"

He got a play acting air about him as he stage whispered to her. "A prowler, where?" He shouted as he added. "This shall not be stood for!" And fell into the snow bank. She couldn't help but laugh, it was all so improbable, being out here, with him, finding he had a funny side.

She poked him in the side and whispered as imperiously as she could, given the situation. "That's not funny." She whirled away from him and just as quickly his hand was on her shoulder again, spinning her back towards him.

"Hey, I'm sorry, I didn't mean to offend." His tone was all contrite seriousness and she couldn't help but shake her head at him.

"It's alright, I really should be going, it's late."

"But of course, where shall I escort you to?"

"I really don't need the trouble of being seen in your company." The moment the words left her mouth she covered it with her hand, aghast at what she'd said. He didn't respond and almost looked hurt by her words, but for only a second, the next he was all stiff, formal politeness. And she almost wished back the rascal of minutes ago. Except that it was easier this way to get him to leave.

He gave a low regal bow as he stepped away from her. "I take my leave then."

Staring at his back as he walked away she wanted so badly to call him back, to apologize and tell him she hadn't meant it the way it had sounded. Instead she kept her mouth shut, knowing that in the long run such an association would only get her in trouble. But as always the what could have beens were there and she couldn't help, but wonder what if…except she was not the sort to attract a Prince, plain and drab. Any attentions he was showing her were because of her initial outburst at meeting him and how they'd met.

So intent on her own thoughts was she that she didn't notice when a shadow slipped up behind her to loom large and menacing.

The cruel hands that shoved her onto stone path were followed by a voice out of a nightmare. And she let out a startled scream.

"You thought you could hide this from me!" Nyriee shrieked, her voice shrill and piercing, reaching a pitch Sereen hadn't thought possible. Sereen tried to scramble away from her, basic survival instincts kicking in.

"You thought you could do this to me, to my daughters! I who took you in out of the cold storm and raised you as my own!" There was something in Nyriee's voice Sereen had never heard before and God willing she never had to again. She was frantic now, trying to get away.

"You thought I would not learn of this deceit! You want to escape me little girl, I'll make you escape!" She'd just noticed Sereen was about to regain footing and stand on her own feet, giving her a better chance to escape.

A shockingly strong hand closed around her neck and hauled her back, dragging her. She continued to tug, trying to get away from this evil creature intent on harming her.

"You will not take from me and mine!"

Sereen could feel Nyriee's nails breaking through the skin along her neck, drawing blood. With a Herculean tug she broke free, spinning to stare at Nyriee.

"This is not about you or your daughters!" Her scream seemed to echo in the chilly night.

A storm was gathering above, full of electricity and anger, at its center seemed to be Nyriee. Nyriee herself looked unlike anything Sereen had ever seen. Her hair stood on end, her features twisted into a hideous sneer, blood coated her fingernails, she looked like a monster come to life. Her teeth looked shockingly pointy, it was the most horrible thing she could ever have imagined. Sereen started to slowly back away, to put distance between herself and this—thing.

Complete revulsion filled her as Nyriee advanced on her, as she could make out an unholy light shining out of her eyes. Before she could contemplate her actions she took off, away from the danger. She barely got three steps before Nyriee grabbed her, wrapping a shockingly strong arm around her throat, cutting off her air.

Nyriee pulled her close, the smell of her breath a rotten stench. "I'll let you go. To hell with Luce, I'll ruin his plans as he ruined mine!"

For a moment Nyriee simply stood there as Sereen struggled for air, to get free, to escape this monster. Then she started chanting in a language Sereen had never hear before, or wanted to hear again, as she chanted she dragged Sereen along, towards the edge of the garden where there was a view down to a waterfall.

Sereen let out a startled scream as Nyriee released the painful grip on her throat and threw her over the side. The feeling of falling overshadowed the pleasure of having air return to her tortured lungs. It seemed like she fell for hours, until at last she landed with a hard thump on something, knocking out all of her air and her unconscious.

***

Kris barely missed running into a lantern pole and pulled himself up short. The garden was empty, peaceful and silent. No sign that moments ago it had been alive with screams.

It had taken several minutes for him to realize the scream had been real and coming from the same place he'd been only moments before.

Tracks were everywhere; he couldn't tell if they were from a new struggle or from his and Sereen's. He started searching. He'd drawn back his hood back up, just in case someone else had heard the scream, he didn't want to be seen and deal with everything that went along with it.

He finally managed to find something that looked more recent and followed it to the edge of the garden. There was a four-foot high stonewall that prevented people from falling over the edge. Here the light was unable to penetrate, but with his superior eyesight he could make out that there was only one set of footprints leading away from the wall with no signs of a struggle.

Curious he looked over the stonewall, but could see nothing in the darkness below. He leaned over further and was off balance when a hideous voice hissed right in his ear as its owner threw him over.

"There shall be no witnesses!" The high pitched voice cackled.

***

The birds were in a titter as they took off. Squawking loudly, they circled around the spot that the Witch had thrown their charge. Burning through them all was a desire to mob her. More pressing though was the need to find the Christmas Star. The Prince would be found as well, but he was secondary to her.

The birds flew through the night squawking out their horrible news. The animals quickly called a meeting. Their decision was to send runners, from the sky and land, to every corner of Christmas Land and hope that they found the pair.

No one believed the Witch had actually killed either of them. Because of her compact with Luce she couldn't kill Sereen without incurring his wrath and it had seemed the Witch had some kind of designs on the Prince. But fallen angels were finicky and who knew when Luce would check up again, and by then Sereen could be dead. Who knew where that hole the Witch had opened up had gone? Their worst fear was that she'd sent her to the mortal realm, a place their poor charge would be woefully under equipped for.

Chapter Three

Sereen groaned, her whole body hurt. Something heavy was lying on top of her, making it difficult to breath. Cold surrounded her on all sides except for the weight on top, which was warm to the point of being hot. She opened her eyes with reluctance, wanting to avoid reality, nothing good had ever happened before when she felt like this. As everything rushed back she wished she hadn't been able to remember at all.

Snow surrounded her on all sides, she could see nothing but creamy white and she couldn't tell what was on top of her. Slowly, she started to make the push to get up, only to find the weight too much. Grunting with exertion she started to shift to get the burden off. Gradually rolling back and forth the mass started to shift and with one last shove she got it to roll off.

It growled when it hit the ground.

She rose quickly; unsure what manner of wild animal had chosen to sleep on her warm body. And stared in horror at the body of his Royal Highness Kris Kringle Claus.

"No, no, no!" This could not be happening, bad enough Nyriee had done this to her, but to the Prince? What had he done to her?

For several minutes she stared down at him, completely taken aback by his beauty. His black hair curled softly, his skin was tan, and he looked very young to have done so many bad things. He was devilishly handsome and the very image of what a Prince should look like. When she realized she couldn't see him breathing she bent down and checked his pulse, maybe the growl had been the last sound from a dying Prince. Thankfully it was steady and strong. Ignoring the heat of his skin against her constantly cold hands she started taking stock of her surroundings.

Wherever Nyriee had sent them, it was beautiful. The view was amazing, making her feel like they were on top of the world. Maybe they were on a mountain. All around them was white and down below were snow-covered trees. The snow was thick, blanketing everything visible in virgin white. Looking around she started to get a dreadful feeling she knew exactly where they were. Nothing visible as far as the eye could see and they were on a mountain surrounded by only trees. There was really only one place they could be.

The Tundra.

The wasteland of Christmas Land.

It was mostly uninhabited. Rumors abounded about strange cults and groups that lived in the nothing land. Supposedly it was where Christmas Land unacceptables went to live, those that didn't fit in or were too malicious to be around normal people. Rumored to be where Santa sent those in need of punishment. One could easily get lost, and never be found. Probably why Nyriee had sent her here.

"Nyriee, what have you done?"

Taking a quick glance towards the Prince she continued her sweep of the land. They needed to get out of the open. The temperatures dropped below those normal in the rest of Christmas Land, quickly, and if out unprotected, it was easy to die. The risk was still there even with shelter, but no matter how slim the chance was it was better than the one they had if they remained in the open. Taking stock of her own clothing and his she found that they weren't as poorly off as she'd initially feared, but they weren't much better.

They were both dressed warmly, though her cloak would do very little to protect her out in this frozen waste. It appeared the Prince was properly attired for the frozen terrain since he'd been off gallivanting before he'd been sneaking through the garden. It was her clothing that would prove the problem. Threadbare and worn, the only decent thing she had was her boots.

The sun had come up not long ago, it must have been later than she'd realized, she hadn't been knocked out that long. Sunlight was wasting however and it was high time to come up with a plan and put it in action.

"Wake up your highness." She gave him a gentle nudge after her previous treatment of him.

As his eyes flickered and finally opened she was confronted with the sight of the deepest blue eyes she'd ever seen. She stared at him shocked. Why hadn't she seen the color of his eyes before? The color of richest blue, like a darkened sky.

Blinking rapidly, he groaned loudly and rolled onto his back staring up at her. "What happened?"

Shaking her head she spoke in the gentlest tone she could, unsure about how his head would be feeling, and what exactly had knocked him out. He could be having issues thinking.

"I'm not sure…" But a horrible suspicion was starting to pull at her. What had Nyriee done?

"Where do you think we are?" Royal decree was in the tone, his dark eyes searching. He'd risen enough to look around. She felt annoyance rising and almost didn't answer, just to spite him.

"The Tundra." Might as well go with the worst idea first. And see if she could annoy him.

He stood abruptly, and nearly fell down. Quickly she placed steadying hands on his shoulders, shaking her head. No doubt about it, he was an idiot male. But for now he was her idiot male to take care of. "Careful, you've got quite a bump on your head. How did you end up here?"

For the life of her she couldn't think of a single reason why Nyriee would have sent him through the hole, she needed him to better her position in life. Nyriee had opened a hole with her magic, to throw her into. It wouldn't benefit Nyriee to send him here when she'd just sent her through the hole because she'd been talking with him.

She found Nyriee's jealousy laughable, now that she wasn't being threatened with death. Why would the Prince, with all those Ladies to choose from pick her? She was plain, boring, and drab, without a single redeeming feature and was a servant to top it off. Perhaps Nyriee was going crazy and should have her head examined. It would explain her bizarre and erratic behavior.

For a moment he simply stared at her, his expression unreadable. "I heard screaming in the garden, not long after I left you. I went to investigate and found it empty. I followed the tracks to the edge of the garden and while I was looking over someone grabbed me and heaved me over."

As she took in his appearance she realized that Nyriee had probably sent him over on accident. If he'd been leaning over with his hood up it would have been hard to tell he was the Prince, all she would have seen was someone that had heard something and come to investigate. She wouldn't have wanted anyone knowing what she'd done. Before last night she would have thought it impossible for Nyriee to throw anyone anywhere, but she'd revealed strength that was at odds with her physique. She'd probably been using magic to enhance herself.

The Prince continued to sit there, looking befuddled. He probably wouldn't be any good for the rest of the day. Telling him her suspicions that Nyriee was throwing people into holes wouldn't help, at least not right now, maybe once he'd recovered a little more.

"We need to get out of the open. As you can see I'm not dressed for this weather."

He nodded woodenly, a glazed look had entered his eyes, and as he turned green she backed away as quickly as possible. He threw up on the ground next to him. For several seconds he stared at it in wonder then she had to run to him as he started to topple. She didn't need him to hit his head again.

Gingerly she lay him down and rolled him onto his side in case he wanted to throw up again. She didn't need the Prince dying in the middle of nowhere. He looked so normal lying on his side, throw-up next to him, looking bedraggled and tired. Taking stock of the situation she came to one conclusion.

Not good.

She needed to find shelter, soon. There were some dark clouds on the horizon and they'd be here before she knew it. The Prince probably shouldn't be left alone, but as she looked around the barren landscape before her she recognized there would be no help for it. She was going to have to.

Giving him one last glance she started on her hunt. It wasn't long before she was thanking every star in the sky that she was wearing her best boots, the most waterproof, snow proof ones she owned. The snow was deeper than she'd thought, but most of it was frozen solid underneath, so she only fell through a few feet. Soon her skirt was drenched and it was hard going.

She was looking for a cave, or an overhang, anything that would provide shelter from the storm that was rapidly approaching. Somewhere that she could get the Prince if he didn't wake up to help her. That head wound was going to need some time, and she would need time to figure out what to do next.

Once his head got better the Prince would be doing most of the deciding, he was after all the Prince. He'd probably want to return to the Palace as quickly as possible, after all he needed to pick a bride. Time was slowly ticking away and wouldn't stop just because he'd disappeared.

Nyriee also needed to be taken care of.

Why in all Christmas Land Nyriee had thought her a threat she had no idea. There was nothing she could have done to capture and hold his attentions. Nyriee would have to be taken care of; her mind was obviously going south in a hurry. A Witch with a bad mind was a recipe for disaster. After Nyriee was gone she had no idea what she would do with herself. It would be nice to have the freedom, freedom to choose how to live.

    She was so caught up by her own musings she didn't notice when she started following paw prints and it wasn't until a small body brushed against her that anything penetrated. She let out a startled yelp and jumped to the side, trying to determine what the threat was.

    The threat was a little snow lion, no more than a cub, more frightened by her sudden outburst than she was by him. It watched her warily for several moments before tentatively coming closer. Finally it got close enough and when she made no sudden movements it rubbed against her and started purring loudly. The rush of relief that poured through her at finding it was something so tiny had her dropping to her knees, wrapping her arms around the cat and petting its silky coat. A minute later several other, fully grown, cats appeared rubbing their warm soft bodies against her. She remained there for several minutes as they warmed her.

    With a shuddering sigh she stood. The largest one shook its head at her and started padding off, the others nudging her to follow him. They led her to a small cave, just right for what she needed.

    She couldn't contain the relief that flooded through her and ran her fingers along each of them in a gesture of thanks. With one last brush of their pelts she turned away and started back towards the Prince, who was still out there freezing.

***

    It wasn't as hard as she'd anticipated getting him down to the cave. Local animals now knew she was here and started helping her. The animals walked down a path and found wood for her to use, making a pile in one of the corners. There were several boughs set by the wall next to the wood for a pallet. She thanked them all greatly, they always were looking for ways to make her life easier and she was pleased with their thoughtfulness. Animals had difficulty remembering such human things as beds and fires, making their remembering all the more poignant.

    She was careful to make sure the Prince was still asleep, unsure of how he would react to the animals helping out. He would already be disoriented and she didn't want to add to it. He might think she'd bewitched them, maybe that she was a Witch. Or that she'd had a hand in having him thrown down the hole.

    Shuddering she turned away from her thoughts. There were more important things to deal with right now, like survival.

    Over the next several hours she got the fire going and the boughs worked like a dream. The animals appeared with meat and somehow a cloak, warmer yet than the one they'd loaned her before. The Prince's was well made and he was dressed warmly enough, the only thing left now was her dress, ill made for such weather. The animals would lend their warmth as well to the pile if it was needed, though hopefully not.

    The Prince still had not awoken by the time the sun was casting its last fiery light into the sky, despite her best attempts. His breathing was strong and steady and he appeared to be okay, but still… She'd found the rock he'd initially hit his head on. It had been smooth and there'd been no sign of blood on it. She hadn't found the courage to run her fingers along his skull and see if she could find the bump, it seemed too personal.

Finally she settled down next to him and fell asleep, exhaustion completely overcoming her. Several warm bodies curling into hers.

***

Kris stared down at the sleeping creature next to him, actually all of the sleeping creatures around him. They'd been piled almost on top of him when he'd woken up. His shock had barely been contained when he'd glanced over at the girl sleeping next to him and found a giant snow lion curled up next to her.

He'd risen slowly in case his head heaved again, but it didn't. For one of the first times in his life he actually thanked his lucky stars that he was an immortal, capable of healing at an exceptional rate. He'd never had a head wound like it before and he planned on never having one again. He was fortunate that she'd been here, or he'd still be out there, frostbitten and concussed.

She'd done a heck of a job dealing with everything while he was out of it. Though he had a suspicion that the animals had helped. He'd heard of people before that could communicate with animals, but he'd never met one before. She'd allowed him time to heal and recover while finding shelter and help.

It was a strange feeling to be so indebted to such a creature. He couldn't seem to stop staring at her either. Silence reigned in the cave, broken only by her delicate breathing and the animals snoring. He'd never met someone like her before. There was something about her that drew him like a lodestone. It was the same thing that had made him notice her in the garden. When he shouldn't have been able to because of the shadows.

He tossed another log on the fire and went to work on the meat sitting there, suddenly ravenous. Some of the animals woke up and he fed them bits and pieces.

It was a companionship that he'd never felt before, even as she slept. She'd done an excellent job, taking charge in a situation that would have sent any of the Ladies he knew into a panic.

Turning back towards her he simply watched her as she slept. Noting how peaceful and young she looked. He could almost imagine her hair was a dark wine red with gold streaks and she looked healthy and alive, like she was pretty, if not verging on beautiful. He shook his head at his own whimsy.

***

Nyriee shrieked at the sky anger and disgust at herself, at the world taking over. The girl was gone, permanently removed from the equation. When Luce found out there would be no end to the torment, the deal would be broken and there would be no further chances.

Her daughters huddled together in the shadows, watching her as one would a mad woman. She supposed she looked as one. Hair standing on end, blood staining her fingernails, eyes with a crazy, hunted look in them. If they only knew the mistake she'd made tonight, in a fit of anger, a fit of madness. There had been too many mistakes lately, the pressure of all of this was getting to her.

As one of them started to stand she snarled at them, making them both cower back into the wall. Let them fear her, what did it matter? The situation was now entirely unsalvageable. Luce would have her back to being his slave again.

She should have known the girl was too dangerous to bring to court, that she'd begin to find her powers. And that she'd use her powers on the Prince! Curse all! She'd been drawing heavily on the girl from the moment they'd arrived, but still her powers had started to come to the fore, like with everyone she'd charmed, it shouldn't have been possible for her to command the attention of everyone like she was. And then she'd ensnared the Prince.

It was too late to recall her actions now, perhaps if her daughters managed to catch the Prince there would be some relief from the hell Luce was guaranteed to put her through.

Chapter Four

Sereen woke up to both small and large bodies snuggled against her, providing a delicious warmth. A smile graced her lips despite the frustration she felt at the fact they had placed themselves in danger. They cared enough to place themselves in danger for her. Just like when she went hunting, there was a natural life cycle and the animals understood when she went hunting she was to be treated as a hunter, just like when the animals were in her presence together no one was allowed to be eaten.

With gentle hands she dislodged several of the little animals and started to rise, only to stop dead when she noticed the Prince was no longer asleep. Had he wondered off? Who knew how the head wound was still affecting him. She quickly started to rise and almost toppled over.

"Let me help." She looked up, shocked, into his smiling face and stunning blue eyes.

With his help she managed to extract herself from the pile of fur and find herself on solid ground again. She quickly let go of the death grip she'd had on his sleeves and took a step to the side, lowering her eyes.

Had they been up she would have seen the consternation in his face.

To give herself something to do she woke all the animals, laughing at the sleepy looks they all gave her and moved them gently on their way. They all tottered around, falling into each other on their way out, several giving her disgruntled looks. Amused by them all she completely forgot about the Prince until he offered her a piece of meat that was fresh off the fire. She accepted it quickly, careful to not touch him.

They ate in a strained silence, both unsure of how to act around the other. They needed to talk about what they planned on doing. As comfortable as the cave was they couldn't continue to stay here.

She glanced up at him just in time to watch him lick the grease off of his fingers. It seemed un-princely, though she wasn't sure what would have seemed more proper in the current situation. The gravity of the situation didn't escape her, nor did the guilt. It was because of her t he was here, if she'd stayed in the rooms instead of trying to find some relief this never would have happened. He'd simply been in the wrong place at the wrong time. What were they going to do?

"Head back to Christmas Land."

Sereen froze, she hadn't said that out loud, had she? "Of course. When should we start, your Highness?"

He shook his head at her, looking almost angry. "As soon as possible."

She felt kind of hurt that he wanted to get back to the Palace as soon as humanly possible, that he wanted out of her company. It was unreasonable and unjustifiable, the Prince had a life, and this was an abrupt interruption. He would want to return to hunting for his wife as soon as possible.

***

It was slow going across the Tundra. Every step they took had them sinking knee deep into the snow. Before an hour was out her skirt was sodden and despite the fact her feet were dry they were cold. When snow started falling Sereen gave an inward groan. At this rate they'd never make it anywhere. The Prince was plodding along; resolve tightening his features, but it was obvious this was wearing on him as well. He looked tired and worn out.

They'd made very little progress. This wasn't going to work. The animals were barely remaining out of sight, he'd made no comment on them, but she wasn't sure how to take it. She'd told them to remain out of sight in case his earlier humor went south. She'd had to admonish them several times, and they weren't taking to it.

There had been several reindeer moving in and out of the brush, looking straight at her, showing their obvious willingness to help out. It was taking a lot of control not to nod to them and let them come over and help out. When she stumbled and almost fell flat on her face, barely catching herself, she'd had enough. The Prince stood a little distance away, oblivious to her fall. A low growl echoed in her throat as she looked him. Enough was enough!

When the animals noticed her distress and they all came forward in a huge bunch, swarming over her. She groaned as they stood around her, cold noses pressing against her. The Prince chose that moment to look back, the look of complete shock and superior knowledge on his face, as if he'd expected this made her want to throw something at him, she barely refrained.

All of the animals started chattering at him, many turning towards her with questions on their faces. She simply shook her head at them, not wanting to give an answer to the questions so obviously being asked in their eyes. Trying to avoid their eyes she ran into the Prince's dark ones. He nodded to her, a regal movement of his head, as if accepting this. That settled the matter, because despite the animals that swarmed around her and the reindeer that wouldn't allow them to take one step forward unless it was with their aid, he didn't say a word.

The rest of the week went on in much the same manner. The Prince seemed to know where he was going, seeming to pick out a path even in the worst of the weather. The animals assured they found food and shelter, and provided for their warmth.

The constant, unending silence on the Prince's part wore on her, making her tense and on guard. After her first several attempts to speak to him, all of which had failed despite her most polite manner, she'd surrendered and started talking to the animals, lest she go mad. Every now and again she'd catch him watching her, but as he said nothing she decided to not break the silence.

He probably thought she was some kind of madwoman, talking to the animals as she did, which would only serve to keep him from speaking to her. It wasn't like she needed him to like her, after all when they got back to the Palace they'd go their separate ways.

They'd been making good time since the animals had been helping. The animals knew all the places that would provide the best warmth and shelter from the elements. They also knew the best, truly easiest ways along the path that the Prince had decided on.

Sereen looked up from the fire at the Prince and sighed wearily, she wished more often than not she'd been sent out here with someone else, someone that would talk to her. This was difficult in the extreme, normally she didn't spend so much time around others and after being at the Palace around so many so ready to talk the silence was nigh unto killing her. She wished she knew what it was that had caused the silence and distance, so she could fix it. The animals were great to talk to, but it wasn't the same as talking to another person.

"Your Highness, would you like some?" She held out some of the meat he'd hunted. The Prince had seemed eager to hunt so she'd let him, the predators had been bringing in plenty, but if he wanted to hunt who was she to stop him?

He looked at her as though she was offering some kind of bug. She turned away the moment she saw the disapproval on his face. Anger simmered low in her stomach. What right did he have to always treat her as if she was dirt? Distantly she was aware of him speaking to her, but she ignored him, feeling petty and wronged. She was shocked when he actually touched her and spun her towards him.

He was in her face shouting and she could feel the simmer of anger boiling into a dark rage. "What's with this your Highness stuff? My name is Kris! Kristopher Kringle Claus! Not your Highness, not sir, not Prince. Kris!"

She narrowed her eyes at him, "Excuse me? When have you ever indicated any desire to be called as such?" She shoved at him. "Listen here you spoiled, rotten, royal rat! I'll call you what I want." Wrenching away from him didn't work, he just gripped her tighter.

"You'll call me by what I tell you too!" His eyes flared with frustration. She glared at him through slitted eyelids wanting nothing more in that instant than to wring his royal neck.

"I'll do as I deem necessary, you're nothing out here but a pain in the butt!" Some small part of her couldn't believe she was behaving like this, yelling at the Prince himself. Irrationally too.

"That may be. But I demand while I'm a royal pain you call me Kris!"

She pursed her lips and stared at him coldly, "Well, *Kris*, is there anything else you'd like, or will you release me now?" Looking pointedly down caused his eyes to follow. Her arms held tight in his grip. He released her immediately. She stood there rubbing her arms for several minutes, looking at him coldly, until finally he turned away from her and stalked into the shadows.

For the rest of the night she didn't see him, she wasn't sure where he'd gone, and she didn't go looking. When he got back the following morning he was sheepish as he spoke to her.

"I'm sorry I got angry with you, I—there's no excuse." He bowed his head, looking very chagrin. For a moment she thought about dragging this out, but decided against it. Whatever had happened while he'd been out there she felt he'd done enough penance. She'd sent out several of the animals to keep him warm and just keep an eye on him. People did stupid stuff when they were mad. One of them had returned chittering at her, it hadn't seemed like a warning, and the little creature had left just as quickly, so she'd left him alone.

"It's alright. Kris." Her voice was soft, conveying the forgiveness and the truth that she didn't hold it against him. "I'm sorry too, I didn't mean what I said." In truth she'd felt terrible about it, wishing she could take it back.

He gave her his devil's grin when he looked up. "I forgive you too."

***

The journey was much more enjoyable after that. They chatted about simple, typically meaningless things, rarely broaching deeper topics. It was easy and light, no longer the stiff formality that had been giving them both headaches.

Sereen had to admit that after breaking the ice the Prince—Kris—seemed like a very nice person. There was plenty of troublemaker and devil in him, but he was clever and smart at the same time. His jokes were typically harmless, meant only to make one laugh out loud, often at him. He had interesting view points on a wide range of things. Often, shockingly enough, his views matched hers, or ran close to them.

Their laughter and conversations had the time passing quickly. It was much more companionable than the silence that had reined for the past week.

She couldn't imagine why someone would want to change him, even if it was Santa. He was perfect the way he was, all of his quirks included. There was an easiness about him that made one comfortable and she could see why it had annoyed him that she'd continued to be very formal with him. He wasn't a formal person in any way, shape, or form. There was a way about him meant to put those around him at ease. He was in many ways an excellent monarch because he seemed approachable, willing to listen and seeming to understand he wasn't perfect.

But if one were kissing all of the maids in the Palace you'd get used to a lack of formality and seem more open, who'd want to be... anyway.

Sighing she laughed at herself, not like it would matter, with all of those women to choose from the Prince—Kris—wouldn't spare a second glance her way. No matter how well they got along out here.

***

Second glance, third glance, fourth, fifth, he wasn't certain how many times he'd been unable to resist staring but it had been too many. It was a good thing she hadn't noticed, or he'd been able to cover it up with making quick conversation. If he hadn't seen it with his own eyes he never would have believed it.

She was beautiful. Those vibrant purple eyes fit her face now, where they'd seemed out of place before. She'd looked the same when they'd first been dropped out here in the middle of nowhere a plain, drab, boring little creature, gradually though—she'd changed, and he knew it wasn't going on in his head.

Slowly, but surely she'd started to look less grey and more healthy and glowing. At first he hadn't been able to believe it, thinking it was some function of his imagination, but it was true. She was becoming a creature of loveliness such as to rival every Lady at the court.

He wasn't sure what had caused this startling transformation and he didn't want to mention it to her, just in case it reversed and he'd found it didn't matter.

She was an amazing person, with interesting views and opinions on every subject imaginable. He found himself frequently taking a stance counter to his own just to argue with her. She argued with him in a manner that was both exhilarating and compelling. Looking alive and vibrant she brought new meaning to ebullient.

Every time he managed to make her laugh it sounded startled out of her, as if it was an unexpected joy. He'd started doing things just to make her laugh, enjoying how it sounded like tinkling bells.

"Kris, look." Her voice cut through his reverie and he jerked his head up glancing at her before looking to where she was pointing. That was another change he'd relished, she'd started calling him by his name. It had taken him blowing up to make it happen, though she probably would have done it if he'd just asked her. The stiff formality of before had grated on him, he'd never been one for formality and certainly never with servants. He hated being treated by his station, hated having it lorded over him.

Off in the distance animals had lined up in rows, watching them. They wandered back and forth, several disappearing and reappearing. When he looked questioningly at Sereen she turned back to him with the same question on her face.

As they continued along the animals thinned out and to his shock he realized Elves were trickling out of the forest in a slow procession and lining up. The reindeer slowed to a stop and he followed Sereen's lead and dismounted.

She walked over to the Elves and dropped a low curtsy. He had to admit he felt very out of sorts, unsure what to do, briefly he considered bowing until all of the Elves turned to him and gave low bows and curtsies.

One of the Elves, an elder one it appeared, stepped forward.

"Your Highnesses, welcome to our humble part of the forest, here in the vast Tundra." He glanced around at his comrades, then spoke again in a voice cracked with age. "Please forgive us, we'd heard rumor, but have not prepared for your visit."

Nothing in Kris's training had ever prepared him for this and as he stood there, struggling to find the proper phrasing, Sereen laid her hand on his arm and stepped forward.

"We beg your pardon sir, for we didn't realize where we were, sad to say we've gotten a little lost." Her smile was warm and generous and the elder melted instantly. He bowed his head to her.

"It's been long since we've had such royal company." Kris noticed how the Elf's eyes were glued to Sereen, not in any rude way, but in awe, almost as if she were the royal company and he an extra. It was unnerving and annoyed Kris that another had seen the beauty that had been his for so long. "We implore you to come and partake of our hospitality."

Kris took the fore, acknowledging her silent push. "We accept your hospitality, it is most gracious of you, especially on such short notice." He bowed to the elder then, who returned the gesture, looking almost surprised he'd spoken.

Sereen's hand continued to rest on his arm, comforting, and when he turned towards her he acknowledged it was a show of her confidence and approval of him. He was swamped with a heady mix of pride and joy over her approval, it seemed like something almost more important than his father's. Grabbing her hand he held it tight as they followed the elder, he wanted her to feel like she was his Lady, even if only for now.

The Elves' homes were strung loosely about a snow bound glade. They were set around in such a way that allowed them to blend in with their surroundings. If you didn't know they were there it would have been a simple matter to miss them entirely.

The Elves gave them a tour of their village, showing them every little nook and cranny. The moment the formalities had been taken care of the Elves had swarmed to them and talked gaily about their village and how happy they were for them to be there. Sereen, he noticed, did an excellent job talking to all of them, she listened and gave the proper answers. If he hadn't known she was a servant he would have thought she was a great Lady of extreme importance.

***

The village was amazing, Sereen loved the way it blended in with its surroundings, adding, rather than detracting from them. All of the Elves were very sweet, wanting to speak with her, but letting her give her attention to everyone that wanted it. They'd all moved on ahead as she stopped for a moment, simply taking in her surroundings.

"Ye be tha' one, don' cha'?" The voice was rough, gravelly with age.

Sereen looked up, surprised. She found herself looking into the face of an Elf of an indeterminate advanced age. She wasn't sure if she'd ever seen such an elderly Elf. "I'm sorry, I don't know what you're talking about."

The wizened one raised an eyebrow in silent question, "Ye don' even kno' what cha' doin' do ya?"

She turned away from Sereen, "Best ye listen close little un it'll be important later." Taking a quick look around the area she leaned close. "Ye be the Christmas Star, the one tha' saves all, fer ye lead them."

With a sharp nod the woman walked away, leaving Sereen to stare after her in bemusement. Who knew what the woman was talking about, when one got to such a mature state they could become disconnected from the real world.

Still thinking on the woman's words she looked up when Kris showed up, some of the animals chasing after him.

Panting for breath he spoke in between each deep breath, his excitement coming through very clearly. "The Elves and animals want to throw a party, in our honor."

"Oh! Did you tell they didn't need to?" Pleasure laced her voice, despite her attempt to control it. She'd never had a party held in her honor, even co-honor. It made her glow in a way that made all those around her stop and look.

"Yeah, I told them." His voice held a stunned quality that caused her to give him a quizzical look, trying to understand. He just shook her head and she let it drop.

***

Tyrissia watched from the shadows as the Christmas Star, Sereen, was lead off by the Prince. Her powers were beginning to show themselves, like how she glowed subtly with a faint light when she was happy. The radiance was the star shining through.

It was highly unlikely that Christabel and Berry had a clue as to where the Christmas Star was, for alls sake last she'd heard the Christmas Star was safe. For some reason the animals weren't divulging any information about her. She'd been shocked when the Elves had said they'd seen a star, traveling with animals that clearly felt it necessary to remain mum about her.

Curious it was that no one knew that she was in the Tundra, excepting the animals, very curious. Christabel and Berry's inattentiveness was inexcusable, who knew what had been happening to the child while they'd been distracted. She'd be having a word with them first chance she got. The one creature they knew they should be protecting closely they'd let slip out and wander wild. What else could have been happening in this child's life while they were busy with their supposedly important matters?

One thing was for certain, luck was on their side or the child would have already been scooped up by Luce and made ready for his dark purpose.

***

It became apparent as she watched the preparations that this wasn't going to be any small time affair, simple with very few frills, the Elves and animas were going all out. Elves and animals had disappeared into the forest and returned with huge logs they'd chopped up. She was pleasantly surprised to find Kris had helped them out.

Food of every different sort was set out. The Elves were vegetarians and the animals obeyed this rule while within the Elves' jurisdiction. The confections they set out were mouthwatering in smell and look.

She helped out where she could, but mostly they ordered her to sit and enjoy. It was pleasant and disconcerting to be waited upon, she always felt like she should be helping out, somehow. The Elves made sure she behaved though and allowed herself to be pampered.

As mid-afternoon neared some of the female Elves and animals appeared and asked her in the sweetest tones she could ever imagine to come with them. If they'd asked anything it would have been hard to say no to them, they were so sweet. When she asked where they were going the Elves merely giggled and declared it was a secret, she'd find out soon enough.

It was a fun surprise, they took her to a hot springs and amid much laughter and giggling told her that they were going to help her look lovely for the feast and party. By the time they were done every inch of her felt clean and she felt pampered within an inch of her life. They dressed her in a magnificent blue dress and plaited her hair with Christmas flowers. She felt beautiful, even if she was somewhat less than. When she made a remark about it the Elves and animals shook their heads at her and declared her lovely, capable of making any woman jealous. She shook her head at them and enjoyed their fun, allowing them an opportunity she had a feeling they rarely got.

A purple and red sunset set the sky awash with colors. Off in the distance one could see the dancing Northern Lights, as they returned to the Elves camp. A bonfire of massive proportions was lighting the entire clearing with an orange glow.

It was a sight to behold with tables set up around the edges of the clearing holding all of the food they'd spent the morning and late afternoon making. By some unknown cue everyone came out of the forest they'd been blending in with.

Opposite where she'd come out of the forest Kris emerged. Obviously a similar treatment had been bestowed upon him. He looked very dashing in a suit of darkest blue, if he was closer she wagered it would throw his eyes into a stunning contrast.

    The females were all on the same side as she, and the males all on the same side as Kris. One of the Elves put a gentle hand on her back and pushed her forward. She took the first tentative steps then seeing Kris being prodded along in much the same manner walked with as much confidence as she could muster towards him, until they met in the middle, right by the bonfire.

    The Elves and animals had come out in the same manner following a few steps behind them. Feeling jubilant and giddy she curtsied to him, feeling as lovely as each of the Elves had said, worthy of a Prince's attention. Kris bowed low to her and took her hand, leading her towards the food. They were the Lord and Lady of the assembly and as such got first pick of the meal.

    Once everyone had gotten food they raised their plates high and thanked the Lord on high for their blessings and the bountiful feast. Logs were set out here and there, some Elves sitting on the ground, some simply standing. Kris found them a spot to sit. They chatted about their afternoon and the things they'd done until the food was gone. Sated and relaxed she leaned back and watched as the Elves and animals finished up their meal.

    More wood was tossed on the fire, coaxing it to a blaze such that any pagan past or present would be proud of. Musical instruments were brought out and they started tuning them up.

    It started out as a low thrum that quickly rose to a roar, a beat impossible to resist, as deep and earthy as life itself. Reaching into the depths of your being and drawing you in. Before long there were Elves and animals cavorting around the fire and the drink was pouring forth from the taps. Laughing she tugged Kris to his feet and joined in the revelry.

She'd never danced before, and she'd certainly never seen any such dancing as she was suddenly a part of. It was a wild cacophony of bodies and stomping feet keeping time with the music. It swept you up in it and suddenly it was a part of you and you it.

She danced around Kris twirling and keeping her feet in time with the music, every now and again his hand would land on her waist and he'd move her about, keeping her in time with him. She'd sway gently with him, then with a giggle she'd twirl out of his grasp, her skirt flaring out largely. It was a pure and joyous movement and it seemed to catch and hold Kris's attention, it seemed he'd looked nowhere else this evening.

Finally worn and panting for breath she begged off the dancing and found a perch to continue to watch the festivities. Blankets had been set on the ground so as the Elves and animals wore out they could rest comfortably and observe until they fell asleep or felt like rejoining. Finding one of these she watched while Kris continued the ancient dance.

She watched, both laughter and somberness filling her, as he danced around the flickering flames. The other females had also vacated the dancing arena, leaving it to the males of their species'.

The animals and Elves danced rapidly around, chasing each other, the animals laughing in their own way. Easily keeping time to the music. Sweat glistened brightly on coats and bodies.

Everyone was smiling and chipper, the cold couldn't touch them, not now. One of the Elves twirled and bowed to her. He was tipsy which made the bowing comical. When Elves got drunk they became rather rowdy and went to extreme lengths to amuse others and themselves. She laughed when he fell to the side, giggling hysterically as he sat there. Some other Elves appeared after a moment and chattered away gaily, giggling at everything the other said. Obviously they were all rather drunk.

It was an amusing sight to behold as the Elves engaged in conversations with the animals and tried to get responses. Kris was the funniest though, dancing around the Elves and animals, it was most undignified for the Prince of Christmas Land. He was prancing around like a pixy, encouraging the others to laugh at him. She hadn't seen him drink much, but it was easy to get giddy and caught up in the entire thing.

His eyes lit upon hers from across the clearing and took her breath away. He looked so handsome, sweat shining on his brow, eyes lit with laughter and fun. Young and happy, everything anyone could ever want. He was the very image of what a Prince should be, not how everyone thought he should be.

She couldn't help but stare at him as he danced his way in and out of the bodies until he stood before her. With a devilish smile he finished coming towards her. He fell as much as sat next to her. She laughed putting her hands out to help him, and prevent him from falling on her. It didn't work.

He landed both sitting next to and on top of her. She couldn't stop giggling, it rolled from deep within, bursting forth uncontrollably.

"I command you to stop." He looked so comical ordering her around that she laughed even harder. "Stop giggling servant, or you'll regret it."

Mere inches separated their faces, taking her breath away. The laughing light had died in his eyes as they stared at each other. Without conscious thought or effort their lips touched.

The revelry continued as they got lost in the kiss. It had revelry all its own.

One of the Elves tapped Sereen and she turned, startled towards him, breaking the kiss. The Elf chattered for a moment at her then moved along. She turned back to Kris, a blush spreading across her features. Instead of making a joke or doing something of that sort, he pulled her against him, resting his chin on her head. It was comfortable and comforting.

They sat there resting peacefully while the revelers continued to cavort. It felt like the calm in the eye of the storm. After a while she fell asleep, lulled by the sound of the dancers and the deep thrum of the music.

Sometime later she woke and stared lethargically up at Kris as he stood. His strong hands reached down and gently helped her up. She leaned into his touch as he supported her. When she stumbled into him he simply swept her up in his arms and carried her.

As she stared glassy eyes up at Kris and she realized she'd fallen in love with him. Madly, deeply in love with him. A Prince.

Tears clouded her vision as she realized what she'd done. She hid her face against his shirt so he couldn't see. It was all fine and well for him to act like he liked her while they were in the middle of nowhere, but the moment they got back to Christmas Town that affection would vanish. She couldn't hold a Prince, and she knew it. What was she but a servant? To a Witch no less.

Despite what affection there seemed to be now, it wouldn't last past them returning to the Palace, she'd be forgotten amid the swirling butterflies. It was a sad thought, but one that strengthened her resolve to enjoy what was happening now, to just live in the moment. She didn't want to think of the future, or even the past for that matter. Right now it was better to just live, once they returned to the Christmas Palace she'd make her plans, for now she simply wanted to be with him. To enjoy the feeling of being in love.

With a smile at him she closed her eyes and returned to resting. It would be nice to come back here, and live with the Elves, they were so amusing and nice, a far cry from the Witch she'd lived under for all those years of her life.

Lulled by the gentle swaying gait of Kris's walk she returned to sleep.

When she woke later she was back in the cottage. The fire burned low in the grate, keeping away the chill of the night. Kris was nowhere in sight. Slowly she got up, unsure of what her intentions were. With a broken sigh she sat down by the fire, torn apart on the inside by her feelings.

She'd fallen in love with a man that was supposed to be married by Christmas, who could never return her feelings. To combat her tears she stared stonily into the fire, waiting for Kris to get back. He must have stepped out to check on something or perhaps someone at the feast. Eventually she must have fallen asleep, because she became aware drowsily of strong hands carrying her again and laying her carefully on the bed.

"Shh, it's alright. Go back to sleep."

She shook her head, wanting to prolong whatever time she had with him, wanting to continue to know his warmth and laughter. He didn't laugh at her contrariness, instead he sat next to her and started talking to her about whatever random thoughts popped in his mind. He spoke about the party and the Elves, about any topic that seemed whimsical and not dealing with serious matters. His words mattered less than the sound of his voice. It was perfect, husky and masculine, comforting and reassuring her back into sleep.

Somewhere along she fell back asleep, lulled into dreams by his voice.

***

Kris stared, defeated, at Sereen. She slept like an innocent child. Too good to be sullied by someone as disreputable as him. He gazed at her wanting to hold onto her forever. When she'd come out of the woods that evening he'd been shocked by how beautiful she'd looked, it was like that drab, ugly duckling back at the Palace had never existed. She looked like someone that deserved to be richly lavished in all the best life had to offer. If he hadn't seen it himself he'd think someone was crazy if they told him about the transformation, but she'd done it right before his eyes. It sounded like a bad line, but it hadn't mattered, as he'd gotten to know her how she looked mattered so little.

Shaking his head he turned away, he didn't deserve her and shouldn't even try. He'd try his best to earn her respect, but even that… he wasn't worth the dirt on her shoes. She was an angel sent straight from heaven, while he was some manner of demon from hell.

Looking back at his life he couldn't find one thing he'd completed that was worthy of her, nor could he find a single admirable thing he'd ever done. But despite all of that he wanted to be worthy of her, wanted her to look at him and not just see Kris Kringle Clause the ladies' man jerk, who'd never done anything worthy. He wanted to be someone she could respect. It was a more powerful desire than anything his father had ever brought forth. She made him want to be things he'd never tried or wanted to be before.

He walked out into the night, staring out at the Tundra, the Elves had finally worn themselves out and fallen into their beds or onto the ground. The fire was almost burned out. Animals lay here and there, sleeping where they'd fallen.

She'd glowed tonight, seeming to shine with an inner radiance. And it had seemed directed at him. So happy and lively, she'd looked at everything with wonder and a smile. All the while seeming to glow with some inner light that only added to the feelings of euphoria present at the feast.

They'd been making good time across the wasteland, if they continued at this pace they'd make it back with a week or so to spare. Maybe he'd still be able to honor his father's wishes, certainly there had to be someone there that would make an acceptable Mrs. Claus.

Someone that wasn't Sereen. She'd make a wonderful Mrs. Claus. He shook his head against the thought, she deserved someone worthy of her. Not him. She deserved someone with an unsullied soul, who wasn't up to all kinds of bad things all the time. Try as he might there were times even around her when he did goofy things, or played pranks on her. She was good-natured about it, but he could see her disapproval as well, her silent shakes of the head. It was part of him he supposed, but it was a learned habit, one that would be difficult to break.

He shook his head, depressed. Sometimes he did crazy stuff just to see her laugh or smile. The first time he'd heard her laugh it had sounded so rusty, but it had held a lilting, melodic quality to it, like the tinkling of little bells. After the first time he'd wanted to hear her laugh as often as he could, it seemed wrong someone with as enthralling a laugh as hers shouldn't laugh. He never asked about her past, to some extent he was afraid of what he might find. It didn't seem she'd been hurt in any physical manner, but you never knew.

Tonight she'd glowed, enchanting him. He'd wanted to go down on bent knee and recite poems and ballads in her honor, to make revelry hazed declarations about her loveliness. She'd taken his breath away when she'd walked into the glade, more beautiful than any Queen. When they returned he'd do whatever he could to get her released from servitude, such a marvelous creature didn't deserve to be forced to serve someone. She deserved to be free.

Despite the warmth and comfort the Elves offered they'd have to get going again tomorrow, maybe they'd have some luck and the weather would be good.

With a groan he turned away from the image of the Tundra to one inside, and much more glorious.

She was blissfully unaware that he watched her as she slept. It felt right though, to watch her as she slept like the angel she was. She always looked so young in her sleep, peaceful. As he stared at her a different thought intruded, she reminded him of a star, lightening up his world, always seeming to glow with life. Even more than an angel. Since her advent into his life everything had seemed more defined, sharper, like everything was more clear. Maybe that was it, even more than an angel she seemed like a star, something that should remain untouched and unsullied by his touch.

Shaking his head over his own whimsy he grabbed his pallet and lay out his bedding. She'd been so insistent that she needed to sleep on the pallet, he forgot often that she had been a servant, with her beauty and actions she always seemed like she should be a Lady. She certainly had the bearing of one. She'd been so shocked when he'd told her that he'd be the one taking the pallet. Such innocent beauty.

Too pure for him. His thoughts flittered away to that kiss, a kiss such as he'd never experienced and decided right then that if she didn't mention it, he wouldn't either. She may have been more tipsy than he realized when she'd done it and he didn't want to learn that the best kiss of his life wasn't even remembered by the other party due to too much drink.

Groaning he lay down and lay on his side, facing away from her. She was nothing like those court Ladies, but suddenly he wished that she was one, at least then he could pretend that maybe he could have her.

Chapter Five

Nyriee smoothed her hand over her face and reached for the vanity mirror—and nearly dropped it.

She was aging rapidly, the maids she'd been drawing upon were insufficient. Despite their number they didn't have half the power the Christmas Star had possessed and were unable to hold her aged beauty to her.

Throwing the mirror away from herself she spun away. Only half noticing the shadow that was forming in the corner of her room. When it finished taking shape she jumped back, startled.

"Luce," It was a breathy curse. "What are you doing here?" Panic and fear combined, making it difficult to keep her composer.

With the walk of a born seducer he walked towards her, and ran the back of his hand along her cheek.

"Wrinkles, Nyriee? I would have thought them below you." His voice was low, caressing, and menacing all the same.

She shuddered under his touch. "My Lord—"

"Sshhh… it doesn't do for you to age so."

She nodded tightly, as he grabbed her jaw.

"What did you say?"

"Y-y-yes,"

"Good. What did you do to her?" He leaned close to her ear. "Where is she Nyriee?" His whispering voice was sharp with menace as his grip tightened painfully. Too late now to change her actions she gulped, staring in horror at him.

"She-she's fine." Under her breath she muttered, "I hope."

"You hope." His voice was soft, hiding vicious steel beneath it. "Careful. Do you not remember our arrangement?"

"Sir, please—she—she was—" Anger flooded Nyriee. Anger at how easily he could reduce her to this blubbering ninny. He made her look the fool. "My daughters were being made fools of, she was taking an opportunity!"

"So you eliminated her?"

"No, milord, I sent her where you can find her. All that remains is for you to retrieve her."

"Ahh. And how am I supposed to know where she is?" When he bit into her ear she jumped and tried to pull away. He continued to bite harder, until she subdued, barely withstanding the pain. Finally he released her. Tears were streaming down her face.

"Forgive me."

"Of course. It doesn't do for you to age so my dear."

She nodded, comforted by his gentle hand on her shoulder, aware of the cruelty contained in that body. Picking up the mirror he handed it to her, forcing her to stare at her reflection. His reflection was also clear in the mirror. Standing like a dark visage over her.

"Perhaps you aren't doing enough about it."

Nyriee shook her head. "I'm doing what I can, the maids here aren't sufficient."

Leaning close he spoke with venom, his eyes piercing hers in the mirror. "Perhaps you should look elsewhere." He cast a glance towards her daughters' rooms. "Maybe you aren't looking in the correct places."

"But what—"

With hands like ice he brushed her hair off her shoulder, "They will never garner the attentions of the Prince, you know this… you should be looking at other…better options."

For one flickering second another image appeared in the mirror, his intent becoming painfully clear. She was young again and the whole crowd was bowing to her.

"I need the spell Luce."

"Of course."

***

Sereen had just gotten up and was wandering around, looking at the destruction from the revelry. Bodies were lying here and there, most of them in a large heaps. It was comical, seeing the Elves and animals piled together. Some had risen, but the majority was lying as if dead, the only hint of life was all the snoring. The fire was still smoldering and probably would for the next couple of days. She'd left Kris in the little cottage sleeping, she wasn't sure what time he'd finally gotten to sleep. It made her feel bad that he kept sleeping on the pallet, it was more comfortable than hers back home, but still...

"Ye need ter be learnin' ter use tha' magic o' yours li'le un'."

Sereen looked up surprised by the gruff voice, to find the same woman that she'd met when she'd first arrived. "What are you talking about?"

The woman shook her head, "Tha' magic wha's runnin' thro' ye."

She stared to shake her head only to be cut off by the woman. "Ye go' mo' magic tha' ye kno' wha' do with." She glanced around the entire clearing. "Suppose, be needin' ter gi'e ya a quick lesson." A sandpapery hand grabbed her and she knew no more.

***

Sereen came to slowly, blinking rapidly at the bright light filtering through the trees. Slowly she raised her head and looked around, wondering where she was. The old woman was nowhere to be seen, nor was anything else. The glade she was in wasn't large and had tree branches interwoven over it, blocking some of the light. Flowers dotted the grass.

Grass! In this glade there was no snow! Despite the fact that all around it, nearly four feet tall was a wall of snow. There shouldn't have been any flowers blooming this time of year and there certainly shouldn't be a clear spot in the middle of a forest, in the Tundra.

"Is magic all righ' little un'. Yo, guess corrrect."

Sereen pushed slowly to her feet and watched the woman hobble across the meadow, in her wake more flowers bloomed. Shock held her still, instead of trying to make a break for it.

"I know wha' cha' thinkin' this taint possible, but wi' magic anyt'ing becomes so. As you'll learn. Now les get star'ed."

Minutes passed as they both stood there watching each other. A bird came and perched on the woman's shoulders and flew off, a rabbit nosed around at their feet. Was it possible she had magic? Magic was a real and vibrant force in Christmas Land, but did she, lowly servant-slave to Nyriee truly have power?

There was only one way to find out.

She didn't know who or what her parents were and just as the woman said anything was possible. The woman could be wrong though. She tamped down her excitement and hope, trying to focus solely on what she was certain she knew.

"What if I don't have magic and you're wrong?"

There was a sharp look in the woman's eyes that slowly softened. "Where ha'e ye been ta no' know ye go' it?" She shook her head brusquely. "No ma'er child, I'll show ye an' gie ye some basics."

There was pure determination in the woman's eyes and Sereen allowed it to sink in that this woman thought she had magic and wanted to train her. Rather than argue with the woman it would be simpler to just accept and when she tried to get her to use magic it would be obvious that she had none.

"Alright, what's your name?"

"Ah, good. Tyrissia, be da name I go'." The woman grinned at her, as if she had some private joke. "Come now, I show ye magic!"

***

Sereen wasn't certain to be horrified or happy when she went through the first set of tests to see how much control she had over her magic and learned that she did, indeed have magic, gobs of it so it seemed. Her control was a little shaky and at first it was only with great difficulty that she found her magic at all, but she could use her magic!

Excitement and anger flooded her at the knowledge. She would be able to break free from Nyriee, she now had a skill that was precious, but on the same note why wasn't she with her family if she possessed such a power?

Such a question had no answer that she would be able to find so instead she threw herself into Tyrissia's training.

When dusk fell she looked towards Tyrissia, expecting to see her point out the path back to the Elves' village, but instead she was informed more work was still necessary before she could return for a bug would bite her, giving her an itch to leave if she did.

Four days later Tyrissia declared that she was acceptable and would at least be able to defend herself reasonably if pushed and allowed her to return to the Elves' homes.

***

When she arrived back at the village she found Kris was waiting for her, having been alerted she was returning. Her heart leapt when she noticed, no matter what she'd been telling her heart it was too late now, it had decided what it wanted and it wanted to get it. She smiled and walked with him into the village, fielding his questions and those of the Elves. They were as curious and talkative as ever, wanting to know if everything had gone well. It seemed Tyrissia had alerted them so they wouldn't worry about her absence. Kris said little about it, turning instead to other subjects.

The evening meal was lain out with gusto and everyone dug in, always appreciative of the food. Late in the meal Kris turned to her and told her the day after tomorrow they would be leaving. At first she bristled over this order, than recognized it for what it was, he wasn't actually ordering, but telling her, giving her an opportunity to stay, to refuse to leave, or tell him it was too soon. She nodded and the meal continued. The Elves had paused for a moment to watch the scene unfold and were obviously satisfied with results.

Tyrissia showed herself as Sereen was preparing her things, packing the new clothing the Elves had given her.

"Yer a gonna be one o' the grea' Ladies, ye kno'."

Sereen didn't startle this time, turning she gave the woman a smile and continued to pack. "Thank you."

The woman watched her as she packed. "Tha' Prince he be in love which ye, ye know."

She shook her head at the woman, wanting to disperse the words before they reached her hopeful heart. "Forgive me, but I don't believe so." He certainly hadn't acted in love with her, he hadn't even asked how everything had gone. Or if she was okay.

The woman let out a cackling laugh and turned to leave, right before she stepped out into the cold she turned back to her, "Ye be a strong un, yes ye be." A gentle smile on her aged face.

Chapter Six

    The Elves had been sorry to see them go and had walked with them quite a ways, laughing gaily when the reindeer had shown up to carry them. He had to admit he'd been sorry to leave. It had been some of the most relaxing and enjoyable time in his life. Everyone knew of his station, but nobody deferred to him, they all expected him to help out here and there, doing those strange odd jobs that lurked everywhere it seemed. Often as not Sereen would help him, smiling merrily when he didn't quite get a task, not in any kind of cruel manner, but because he just didn't know how.

    Her laughter had made every task easier, when he wasn't around her he wanted to find her, just to be near her. She made everything bright and cheerful, everywhere she was there were always countless Elves and animals, simply basking in her glow. She'd made no mention of the kiss, either not remembering or having forgotten it. Either way when he thought of it he deflated some. He wished she'd give him some sign she remembered as well as he, but instead of forcing the issue he tried to remain gentlemanly.

Kris turned to glance at her and realized she'd stopped. He pulled the reindeer up and looked back at her, then looked to where she was staring.

***

Set in the distance was a cottage, almost unnoticeable against the backdrop of white and green. It had been built to add rather than detract from its surroundings. It blended in with the surrounding countryside.

Something tugged her towards it, some inexplicable force, pulled her towards the cottage. She didn't bother to look and see if Kris was following her as she continued towards it. About ten feet away from the cottage she pulled the reindeer to a stop and sat staring at the cottage.

A strange fear filled her, combating her curiosity. Her eyes sliding closed with a shudder. She felt torn inside, afraid of what she might find. She was on the edge of a precipice, about to fall into the abyss. This was one of those life changing decisions, she could feel it in her bones, vibrating deep within. If she went forward something would change, if she went on her way, left it behind, things would go on much the same, but would she wonder forever what she'd passed up? What opportunity had she missed?

"Are you going to look?" His voice vibrated through her, drawing her from her confusion. Opening her eyes she glanced over at him. Snow was dusting his hair, the cold had placed a healthy pink on his cheeks, his blue eyes were sparkling, showing such life. With him at their side one could feel like they could do anything. They could fly or rule the world, be anything, do anything.

It made her ache inside. Knowing she wouldn't be the someone that would fly beside him and rule the world with him. The kiss always weighed on her mind, even when she'd been training it had been there, but he'd not said a word and it was easier to just let the subject lay. He probably thought he'd made a grave mistake and didn't want to remember it, to dredge up the memories. After all who would want to admit to kissing the ugly servant, even in the heat of the moment? Better to leave it alone and not ruin the ease they'd found.

Turning back towards the cottage she noticed that no lights were on, no smoke curled from the chimney. But it didn't look abandoned…it looked lonely, like it was waiting for something. Or someone. Staring at it she realized that for whatever reason she was going to take a look at it, she wasn't going to let this pass, she wanted to find out what drew her in about it. Why did it call to her?

A burning desire filled her, pushing the trepidation she felt into the furthest corner of her mind.

With quick ease she slid off the reindeer, noting Kris mimicked her actions.

"You don't have to come with me. Who knows what's waiting in that cottage."

He gave her a disbelieving look. "You think I'm going to allow you to go in there alone? You're as crazy as—as I don't know what. Come on, let's go." Reaching out he grasped her hand, tugging her towards the cottage, leaving her no choice. Strangely she appreciated him taking charge, using his impulsiveness to overcome the mental obstacles she was rapidly building in her mind.

When they got within two feet of the door she felt them pass some kind of a barrier. She wanted to stop and investigate, wanted to understand how she felt a barrier, but Kris tugged her along.

When they reached the door they pulled to a stop and he turned towards her, giving her a questioning look. "Well?"

She cocked her head to the side and raised an eyebrow, "Me? Mr. Trouble, I don't think so. You're the one that was all gung ho. You open it."

Shaking his head he declared, "You're the one that wanted to stop here, but you've piqued my curiosity." Moving her forward, but keeping his hands on her shoulders he pushed her to the door. It was comforting, letting her know that she wasn't alone, despite the cold running through her blood. His hands were warm, giving her something to focus on.

Reaching out she pushed the door open, surprised by the electric tingle that shot up her arm. She half turned towards Kris, for—something, something he gave without being asked. She supposed it was simply reassurance.

Her first steps into the house were tentative. Instead of shouting out to see if anyone was there, she remained silent. The cottage was solemn, encouraging one to silence, rather like a graveyard. It was freezing inside as well. Dust lay on every surface, but so did a sense of waiting, of anticipation. It was waiting for something. Did it ever worry it may never come?

She kept her steps light and silent and Kris followed suite, keeping the silence. His hands had slipped from her shoulder, to one resting warmly on her side, reminding her he was there.

Their footsteps sounded eerily as they walked.

The cottage had a loved feeling to it. Those that had lived there had loved, and it had spilled abundantly into the house itself. She could almost hear laughter and giggling, almost see the bright, lively colors of what had been there before. It was all gone now, but its echo remained. All that was left was the reigning silence and feeling of things lost.

Despite that, or maybe because of it, she felt a strange connection to the house, for all of its bizarre Halloween feel. It felt as if she'd been there before, though she tried to dispel the feeling that had her caught in its strangle hold.

When they reached a stairway leading upstairs, despite the increased pressure from Kris's hand she went up. Curiosity held her tight in its grip, she wanted to explore all of the house and understand why she felt such a connection to it.

The landing was small, the walls covered in pictures of people, the most frequently occurring were those of a woman and a child. She stopped and peered intently at them, one could follow the growth of the child in the pictures, from an infant until she was about three. Then all the pictures ceased. There were no more of anyone, there was a gaping hole where it felt like there should be more. For some reason tears pricked at her eyes as she stared at the blank spot, something had happened to the family that had lived here.

Something that had ended all the laughter.

A crash outside drew their attention. When they reached the front door Kris pushed her behind him and continued forward. Despite pushing she couldn't get him to let her go first. The instant he stepped the few feet from the cottage her eyes went wide with realized horror.

"Kris, no stop!" She was reaching after him despite the distance that separated them, trying to pull him back, going across the barrier again had triggered something.

She chased after him unable to do anything as Kris continued to run, chasing the tracks that some creature had made on the pure snow. In dawning terror she realized they were nearing a cliff, and Kris hadn't noticed.

"Kris stop!"

He paid her no mind, continuing along the trail.

"KRIS, STOP!" She howled as he finally seemed to realize she was there and slowed to stop, only to slip on some ice, hidden beneath a layer of snow. His eyes met hers as he tried to find purchase on the slippery surface, continuing to slide towards the cliff, unable to stop. They both knew what would happen next, even as tears welled and streamed down her cheeks. He made one last desperate attempt to find a hold—

And disappeared over the edge.

Chapter Seven

Tears streamed down her face as hopelessness filled her. He lay broken and battered and she couldn't do anything. She'd followed as safely as she could on a small path along the cliff's side, pushing herself to her limit to make it down to him. Frustrated, she made a keening sound, wanting to take her anger out on the world. As she stood there wanting nothing more than to do battle against the world the magic started to fill her, brought to the fore by her emotional tumult.

Tyrissia hadn't shown her how to heal; it had all been about defense, protecting herself. But she couldn't stop herself from kneeling and placing her hands on his chest. Sending the awesome power out from herself and into him. Her anger, her desire to keep him in this world burned through her, flooding through her and into him.

She forced her power into his body until exhausted she collapsed next to him.

***

Kris woke up feeling like he'd been run over by a sleigh. His mind unwilling to accept he was still here, among the living. It wasn't possible that he was still here. His head was back, staring at the cliff he'd just come from, no one should have survived that fall. Something next to him moaned and he moved quickly, trying to figure out what was next to him. His jerking about didn't make his body feel any better, but did allow him to figure out who was next to him,

Sereen lay next to him on the snow, looking as if the Death Reaper had come for her. Only the steady rise and fall of her chest gave him some comfort that she was still with him. Slowly he got up and looked around, finding the path he assumed she must have taken down to him. The animals were burrowed around them, licking at Sereen's face plaintively trying to wake her up. And the reindeer stood near. He wagered he'd be able to get her on one, despite the aches running through his body and navigate a safer way up the path.

***

Kris took careful care of her for the next couple of days. The animals were a huge help, bringing him food and wood when she came down with a fever the first night. He'd never felt so stressed out and inept in his life as he tried to keep her temperature down. Nothing in his life had ever prepared him for this and by the time her fever broke on the third night he was ready to give up everything and be done, he simply wanted her better.

He came awake, startled. Blinking several times he realized that he was staring into Sereen's vivid eyes, looking cognizant and cool to the touch. Before he could think of his actions he reached out and enveloped her in a hug, the relief coursing through him overwhelming. He'd been so worried about her, so afraid.

They stayed two more days to make sure that she was fully recovered, Kris didn't want a repeat of the last week. That and if it did happen again there wouldn't be such easy protection for them. Sereen seemed fine with this plan, but very subdued. Every opportunity it seemed she was pushing to get him ready to go. There was impatience in her every action and when they left she seemed almost jubilant, like a large weight had been lifted from her shoulders. He wondered what it was that had left her in such a hurry to get out of the cottage.

Chapter Eight

The closer they got to the Christmas Palace the more melancholy she got, and the quieter. Kris had noticed her mood the instant it started to appear and proclaimed they'd spend one more night out in the open. She shook her head at him. They could have made it to the Palace by nightfall, and they both knew it. But once Kris had decided they were staying out one night more she'd crumpled to it. Despite the fact she was going to leave, the selfish center of herself wanted to be around him, keep him all to herself for as long as she could. One more day was just going to make it harder to let go.

They set up camp together, working side by side. There was a tension between them that hadn't been there before. Had he guessed her intentions? She shook her head to dispel the thought, he couldn't know, there'd been nothing she'd done or said to indicate what she planned. The plan wasn't even a real plan. She tried to act relaxed and calm, like everything was normal, and knew the act was failing miserably. As much as she could she tried to hide her face and expression from him, lest he guess.

She'd never found the opening to tell him about Nyriee and had decided to just deal with the matter herself. With her new found powers she was sure she could deal with whatever Nyriee sent her way. Then Kris wouldn't have to bothered with the problem, though by the way he'd been acting lately she wondered if he'd even care.

***

As they got closer to the Palace Kris felt an overwhelming desire to go as slow as possible, to take a detour, maybe one that took years. He didn't want to return to life back at the Palace and he didn't want to have Sereen there. He wanted to hide her away and keep her away from the prying eyes and hands of the dandies at court. It was unreasonable and every second it was building in him. As he went he figured out what the exact emotion was that assailed him, jealousy, in its purest form. He was jealous there was someone out there that was good enough for her, someone that would end up with her, would hold that pure heart in their hands, someone that wasn't him.

Just as he'd seen the Palace in the distance he'd made a split second decision. He'd turned and asked her if they could stop for the night, knowing if they continued they'd make it back before nightfall. He wanted one more night with her, it didn't matter what he was missing back at the Palace. He wanted her all to himself one last time. It was obvious the kiss they'd shared hadn't meant a thing to her and all he could do was try to accept it and enjoy what time he had with her before they returned and she disappeared.

It had been a pleasant surprise when she agreed. If she'd looked relieved, or even pleased, he chalked it up to his imagination and wishful thinking.

Throughout the day he watched her looking for—some sign, he didn't even have a clue what it was. She looked unhappy and he wondered morosely if she was regretting her choice to spend one more night out in the open. It was obvious she was trying to appear that whatever was bothering her wasn't, but it wasn't working.

The animals helped them set up camp, making it quick and efficient. Kris glanced around when he got the fire started, trying to figure out where she'd disappeared to. Picking out her tracks in the snow he quickly tracked her, until he got within hearing of her melodic voice. It washed over his senses in a gentle breeze of tinkling bells. For a few minutes he stood there simply absorbing the sound, a sound that all too soon he'd be deprived of. Then the tears in her voice broke through to him.

"Little one, I know that what is out here isn't real. The moment we get back he'll forget me, and—I just don't know." She looked off into the shadows, but Kris was struck hard by her words.

Words sticking in his brain like a blazing neon sign, before he thought twice he was stepping out of the trees he'd been hiding in. She looked up startled and horrified at him. At first he felt rejected then remembered he'd just broken in on her making a confession to an animal that had flown away startled by his abrupt entry, he would probably have worn a similar expression.

***

Sereen gaped at Kris, he'd heard ever word of what she'd said to the little bird, she could read it in his face. Before she could decide whether to act outraged or—he was on her, standing mere inches away from her.

Almost soundlessly his name fell from her lips, "Kris."

"I won't forget you when we get back."

She shook her head, a sad smile flittering at her mouth.

He grabbed her hands, bending down so he could look into her eyes. "I promise I won't forget you."

A fat tear rolled down her cheek. "Don't promise me that Kris, you can't—"

With tender hands he cupped her face, wiping the tear off her face. "Don't look so sad, I promise you, I'm not going to forget you, no matter what. I'll swear if you like."

She gave a choked laugh, "No, don't. Kris…" She sighed, reached up and put her hand over his, where it rested on her face. "It's alright, if you say you won't forget, I believe you."

Wrapping her in a hug he whispered in her ear. "I won't forget you, ever. No matter what happens."

She buried her head against him. "I trust you."

The problem was, did she trust herself to not get him killed? As she leaned against him she realized the unavoidable truth, it wouldn't matter if he remembered her, because she wouldn't be around. She'd disappear. She didn't want him torn between two worlds, she wanted him to live his life, in his world. If she stuck around he'd get hurt, it had been her curiosity that had lead them to the cottage. And if she stayed she'd try to distract him from his wife hunt, no matter how nobly she tried not to. She didn't want to watch Kris marry another woman, no matter who it was or how good a person. But she loved him and wanted him to be happy. It would be a simple matter to disappear and despite his words, she knew he'd forget.

She'd deal with Nyriee who'd would be a threat to his happiness then disappear, leaving him safe from the trouble that always seemed to come in threes.

The first two had come because of her and she didn't want him to be around her for the third. Whatever the trouble was after her it couldn't be allowed to touch him. Besides who was she but an ugly duckling? Too grey and drab for the attentions of a Prince.

A tear rolled down her cheek as she realized he'd promised only to never forget her, nothing about returning her feelings, all too many of them. Relief coursed through her. At least he hadn't heard the other piece of her confession, her secret was safe, he expected only friendship. And knew nothing of her love.

Chapter Nine

The moment they entered the Palace people stopped and stared at them. She gave Kris credit, he didn't act like she was just someone tagging along. They walked together through the town and into the Palace. Once people got over their astonishment they swarmed to the Prince. She was quickly pushed aside, no one paying her attention. Several people gave her askance looks, but were swiftly caught up in the horde.

Before long they'd pressed Kris forward and she was lagging behind, the evil genie on her shoulder making her follow at a distance, to watch as he was swept into Christmas Hall and more people joined the throng. In the Hall he was led up to the thrones and stood there, a bright smile on his face. For a second she thought he looked as if he was searching the crowd for something, but she quickly dismissed the thought. Who did he have to look for? He had everything right there.

As Sereen watched Kris the undeniable truth settled hard at the pit of her stomach.

She was going to let him go, she wanted him to be happy and safe.

He'd already almost died twice because of her, she had to let him go, despite the fact it would tear her apart. She was dangerous to him. She didn't want to be the reason he no longer ran wild, couldn't bear the thought of a world without his laughter and easy ways. It would be a sad world indeed, better to love him from afar than get him killed by being around her.

With a sad smile she disappeared into the crowd. He'd forget her anyway, with all the Ladies around. No matter his promise, how could she compete?

***

A ball was held that evening and despite Kris's fractiousness and need to find Sereen he couldn't escape the expectation of his appearance. He didn't want rumors going around about her, casting an ill light on her. To make her irrevocably tied to him. The dark part of him burned to do just that, but he couldn't taint her with his own greed.

He looked up, glaring, when someone barged into his room without knocking. He'd specifically told everyone he wanted privacy. It quickly disappeared when he noticed it was his father standing there. Bowing low he spoke in a gentle tone.

"Father, forgive me if I've worried you, it was not my intent."

St. Nick merely shook his head. "I knew you were safe, I would have been aware if it had been otherwise."

Kris merely nodded, he still felt bad that he'd barely spared a thought to his father during his trip, who had surely been worried about his only son.

Santa wandered around Kris's room looking here and there, picking up little knick-knacks and inspecting them for several long seconds. The silence hung thick and heavy. When his father finally looked at him, Kris raised an eyebrow in silent question. Instead of answering Santa looked away and continued to look around the room.

"I don't know where you've been, nor why you left, but you're back now." His father's voice startled him and as did the topic. "That girl, who is she?"

Kris opened his mouth to reply, only to snap it closed again, refusing to answer.

Instead of forcing Kris to answer Santa continued, "If you don't want to continue with this Kris we can stop, we'll move on. We'll send them home."

Kris stared aghast at his father. It had seemed back in October that his father had been set on forcing him to marry someone. Now this.

"Father, I—" He looked away into the night. There was only one person he could even think of marrying and he didn't deserve her, couldn't dream of holding her, no matter her current feelings which seemed to be indifference towards him. Turning towards his father he spoke with more conviction than he felt. "I want to continue this, I still need to find a bride."

His father gave him a searching look, but instead of commenting he simply nodded. "Yes, of course. Let me know when you've made your selection."

He watched as his father started for the door, his stomach turning in circles, wanting nothing more than to say he'd made a mistake and already had someone suitable picked out. Opening his mouth he was about to speak when his father turned.

"By the way Kris, who *was* the girl with you?"

***

As she watched Kris from a reasonable distance away someone bumped into her. Turning she was shocked to find Santa Claus himself standing next to her.

"Forgive me my dear, Sereen, right?"

A smile of brilliant warmth lit up her face. Making her look akin to an angel, a glow surrounding her.

"Yes, sir."

"I've been looking for you, child."

Her eyes widened with surprise, "Oh, I'm sorry. I haven't received word. I—"

He held up his hand to silence her.

"Shush child, I haven't sent for you. I wanted a chance to bump into you. To catch you without warning."

She cocked her head, curious.

"You are very young. You are the one that traveled with my son, correct?" Curiosity was reflected in his voice.

She nodded quickly, "Yes."

"He speaks quite highly of you."

"Oh," She flushed prettily. It merely added to her beauty. A rare and most becoming child. "I didn't—"

"Of course child, now that I've met you I must admit the reason is quite clear."

140

"You flatter me." Her eyes were bright, sparkling diamonds in a pale, beautiful face, that had flushed red with embarrassment.

"Ahh, but not too much. You must come visit with me sometime m'dear."

"Of course, merely inform me." Her voice was sincere and warm.

"At once."

He glanced out towards the assembly, observing how her gaze followed his to Kris. "He'll find a wife yet, despite his long absence."

Her smile became tight as she looked out at Kris, biting her lip. "Yes."

Santa wasn't quite ready to turn her loose yet, instead he chose a different method of attack, "Should be a full moon on Christmas Eve this year."

Merely nodding she continued to look out over the crowd.

"It will be a simply stunning wedding, something for the ages to remember."

A frightened look had entered her eye as she turned to him. "Has he mentioned someone?" There was a note of panic in the tone, belying her desire, he was sure, to appear unaffected. And he felt his compassion rise.

"No, but soon I'm sure."

Nodding tightly she took one last look to where Kris was standing and spoke in a voice barely above a whisper. "I have to go," She had the frightened look of a doe ready to bolt, with a tightly lashed pain in her eyes.

It didn't stop her though from turning and giving a genuine smile, such to rival the Fairy Queens. "It has been nice to meet you." Honesty reverberating through her voice.

She turned with a wave and attempted to disappear into the crowd. But one such as her would always stand out, no matter where she was.

Santa shook his head as he looked out over the group he'd been entertaining for the last months. He wasn't sure why his son bothered when the most precious jewel of them all was fleeing down the hall

He could see quite easily why his son spoke so highly of her though.

Sereen.

Christmas Star.

That was its exact translation in the old language of Christmas Land, kept alive only be the most devoted and by those out in the Tundra. Something tickled at the back of his memory. Something he knew he should remember. It danced there just out of reach.

Shaking his head he turned to watch his son, wishing his memory was what it once had been.

***

Questions concerning Nyriee turned up one unanimous answer. She and her daughters had left during the night weeks ago and a new Lady had moved into their old rooms. The Lady was late coming, but according to the servants she was quite a beauty.

"Wouldn't surprise me none if that one caught the Prince's eye. She's a beaut', seems to be fair decent so far too. Much better than that witchy woman what occupied them rooms before her."

Every servant she talked to had the same tale. The new Lady was very beautiful and a lovely person in general, everyone sang her praises. She was maybe a little cold, but otherwise... Maybe the Prince would find her and fall in love, if she was as good a person as everyone said she'd make a wonderful Mrs. Claus and she'd appreciate Kris with his sweet heart.

Sereen had to meet this woman that Kris would probably do well to make his wife, who would place him forever beyond reach. Quickly she moved down the halls to the rooms. When she reached them she straightened her dress and smoothed her hair. Undoubtedly she looked like a plain servant. They'd been good enough to give her a bath and some clean clothes. Though... she'd been unable to figure out their curious looks though, and the looks she'd received from the men in the halls. As she stood there she felt a strange tug at her magic, but quickly severed the link, no one needed to draw on her power, it was hers to do with as she pleased. And so rude to draw from another without permission according to Tyrissia.

For a flittering moment she wondered what she was doing. What had pushed her to want to meet the creature that would replace her in Kris's affections? She had no reasons to meet her, it would only prolong this and reveal what she could never be.

Before she could change her mind she rapped on the door. She heard someone moving around inside and after a brief pause the door opened revealing a stunningly beautiful woman. She had white blond hair, tanned skin, and piercing blue eyes the color of ice. With the feel of it too.

"Why, hello. Are you new here?" Her voice was sweet, but something was missing. She couldn't put her finger on what it was.

The Lady was dressed immaculately in a dress the same color as her eyes, making her into a stunning picture of purity. Sereen's dress was a dark red, matching the color of her hair. It was anything but innocent. Trimmed with gold braid it clung in all the right places. It was the dress of a Lady, a Lady on the hunt. Why the servants had chosen this dress was beyond her. It wasn't like her at all. She was a servant, one with boring looks. When she'd asked one of them they'd shaken their heads and said simply, "Have you looked?" She'd given them a puzzled look, but said nothing. She still wasn't sure what they'd meant.

"Please come in, I insist."

Sereen smiled congenially and accepted her invitation. "Thank you."

The room itself looked much like it had before, except much more Christmas oriented. It looked like a hurricane of Christmas colors had appeared in the room. The affect was overwhelming, but made the Lady stand out in her more muted color. Turning towards her Sereen spoke, "What was your name? I'm afraid I didn't catch it."

Surprise showed on her face. She spoke in soft tones, like she was afraid to speak too loudly, "Oh, forgive me. It's Nyssa. Would you like something to drink?"

Nyssa, it was a pleasant name, fitting for the woman before her. "No, thank you."

"Oh, I must insist. And what is your name?" Her back was to Sereen as she poured drinks, something strange emanated from her. She appeared timid and rather shy, but there was something about her that seemed like this wasn't who she was. Suddenly Sereen had to get away, something was wrong here, she just wasn't sure what it was yet. It reminded her of the tug she'd felt as she stood outside the room. It seemed imperative that she get away and warn Kris there was something wrong with this Lady.

"I really must be going Nyssa, but thank you for the offer."

As she turned to leave her eye caught on a flash of twirling red in the mirror.

She stared in shock at the image.

It was her and she was beautiful.

Not in the cold way of Nyssa, but in a warm vibrant way that spoke of laughter and love. Her body so grey before was alive with color, her hair, her complexion. She looked healthy and alive, like a goddess brought to life.

She was so distracted she didn't notice Nyssa had come up behind her until it was too late and realized to her horror what was under the illusion.

As the butt of the knife she couldn't avoid came down she whispered—

"Nyriee."

***

Nyriee stared down at Sereen, now lying on the floor. She'd gotten lucky, so lucky. Now she had the means of getting rid of Luce once and forever. But before she turned her over to his waiting hands, she could draw some power from the Christmas Star. Drawing on her own power she sent tendrils out to wrap around Sereen, searching for her magic. Once she found it she made to place the tendrils in it as she had so long ago, only to run into a solid wall. Try as she might she couldn't push through it, it was as solid as stone.

She stared down at her in consternation. How had she learned to control her powers? There should have been no one that could have helped her. The Prince certainly never would have. Had someone guessed who and what she was? No, they would have protected her, guarded her, kept her safe. For certain she wouldn't have been here if it was known. It was probably an accident, the girl couldn't have had such control.

Glancing around the room she knew she needed to get her out of here. She could place her with her daughters, carefully hidden, until Luce came and retrieved her. A sinister smile curved her lips, for the Christmas Star's sake she hoped Luce could break those barriers, that they were just an accident, otherwise it would do no good for Luce to have her. He'd be better off killing her, as long as she lived she was a threat. She could escape and kill him.

Laughing she made sure the girl was still knocked out, what would Luce do if he found he couldn't break her?

Chapter Ten

The room had the damp feel of a basement or cellar. There was a small window in one corner that appeared to lead to the outside, but otherwise it was entirely dark. It smelled musty, and was undoubtedly rarely used, wherever it was. Hopefully Sereen thought she was still inside the Palace, she couldn't imagine Nyriee wanting to leave the Palace any longer than she had to, particularly with the Prince now in residence.

With a groan she plopped her head in her hands. Kris. Nyriee's intent with her new look was perfectly clear, she was planning on winning the Prince, and with her good looks and seemingly perfect character there was little chance of it not happening.

A cold hand touched her shoulder and she let out a yelp as she jumped.

***

Kris looked out over the assembly of Ladies, wishing that he was back in the Tundra with Sereen. None of these women compared to her, in looks or grace. Already he was weary of them and their constant fawning, hanging on his every word, always looking at him expectantly. It was exhausting, making him wish for the easy company he'd been with for the last month and a half. It had been relaxing, she'd expected him to be nothing more than what he was, making him burn to be something more, but relaxing him at the same time. All of these women made him want to do outrageous things to see how far he could push them.

He hadn't seen her since they'd arrived, making him wonder what had happened to her. Several theories had come to mind, but until this appearance was over he couldn't escape. The moment this was over he was launching a full scale assault and finding her.

He was just formulating a brilliant plan that involved the Ladies hair when a soft hand landed on his arm. At first he thought Sereen had reappeared, but the hand was too tan. Unlike Sereen's, as was the Lady herself, so unlike Sereen's vibrant warmth.

This Lady was ice. Dressed in a dress the color of ice she stood regal as any Queen. White/blonde hair was upswept, falling down her back in a brilliant cascade. Her eyes were the same pale blue as her dress. He was taken aback and stared at her for several seconds before he remembered himself.

With a low bow he requested her name, "Forgive me my Lady, I don't believe I've had the pleasure of making your acquaintance. I am Prince Kristopher Kringle Claus."

Her smile was pure feminine pleasure as her hand wrapped around his arm. "Of course your Highness. I am Lady Nyssa Danta—" She stammered for a second and flushed, endearing herself to him. "I arrived late to the court and you have been absent these many days."

Opening his mouth to defend himself, she shushed him effortlessly.

"It's alright your Highness, I'd have been a sorry sight had we met before. My estate is somewhat poor and I needed time to acquaint myself with the practices of the court. I've never been you see."

Her voice was soft, gentle as a whisper. She mesmerized him, the first Lady he'd met that seemed to be someone he was looking for.

"Of course. Have you had an opportunity to tour the grounds then, milady?"

She blushed shyly, shaking her head. "I'm afraid I'm not much for gentlemanly company."

He shook his head at her words. "Then they must all be blind, come allow me to give the grand tour."

With his words and her hand firmly planted on his arm he swept her away to show her all the Palace's regal beauty.

***

Sereen stared in dismay at the two crones in front of her. Both were bent and gnarled with age. Time had done her worst on these two. She felt true pity for them, no one deserved such horrors as had been bestowed upon these two. And being stuck in a dank, damp cellar no less as well. It shocked her. Who would want to hurt two old women?

It had startled her mightily when the one had lain her hand on her arm. They were now peering intently at her, trying to look into her. Their eyes were probably going as well, the poor things.

"Sereen?"

She stared in dismay at the pair as suddenly it became clear and she recognized them all too well. The voice was age roughened, but it was too apparent who the underlying tones belonged to.

"Oh, Christmas! Areenie? Floria?"

They nodded their heads and for several minutes they all stood there absorbing the shock. Sereen was the first to break the ominous silence.

"What happened to you?"

Dark looks were exchanged and the one Sereen was certain was Areenie buried her face in her hands.

"She did this to us."

A sob tore from Areenie, and Floria patted her gently on the back, clearly the strong one now after their mother's betrayal.

"How?" She felt like she was going to fall down.

What mother would do this to her daughters?

She already knew, a Witch. A Witch would do whatever it took to achieve her ends, with no thought to the lives of others. It was a cold way to live. It was no way to live. They shared a quick look, some understanding passing between them. Then they started speaking rapidly interrupting each other.

"She drugged us. What reason did we have of suspecting our own mother? She didn't knock us completely out, then she cast some kind of a spell over us—"

"It drained us, she took all of our life—"

"Our youth!"

"It was so fast it knocked us flat."

"And we could do nothing."

"When we woke we were old, it looked as if we'd lived centuries. And we were here, wherever this is."

"Did she say why?"

They shared a bitter laugh. "Of course. We weren't living up to her high expectations and as such we didn't deserve the gift she'd given us. She said our failure in not garnering the Prince's notice left her no choice."

Sereen shook her head. Nyriee's plans had merely changed. It had never made sense that Nyriee would have one of her daughters marry the Prince, what real power would she get from the marriage? Better that she marry the Prince herself and hold all the power than use puppets, like her daughters, who might not follow her orders to the letter.

She had to get out of here and warn Kris about Nyriee. Nyriee'd set herself up perfectly. With all the fakes wandering around Nyssa would look like an angel, an angel of mercy sent straight from heaven to be his Mrs. Claus. Groaning she turned away cursing herself, like a ninny she'd cleared the path for her.

Gnarled hands swept through her hair. "So beautiful, what did you do Sereen?"

Distractedly she shook her head trying to think. "I'm not sure what happened—"

Realization hit as she stared into the shadows. Realization at what must have been happening. The Witch must have been drawing from her, just like she'd tried to do when she'd gone and seen her. All this time, she'd been drawing upon her. That was why she'd always felt so much better when she was away from the

Witch, so much more alive. And being grey ensured no one would ever want her. Except it had almost backfired, when the Innkeeper's son had asked for her hand. It made sense now why the Witch hadn't wanted her to go with him. What didn't make sense was why the Witch had tried to kill her if she was drawing life from her.

Of course. She'd interfered with her work on the Prince, and now that they'd returned she'd needed her out of the way so the Prince didn't continue to look at her, didn't compare the two of them and find something lacking in her. She'd also created Nyssa, the perfect creature, allowing her to easily begin getting the servants on her side. Everyone knew servants were the ones that came in contact with the worst sides of humanity. It was the same no matter what species or where you were. So if by chance, as so many did, the Prince or Santa inquired, she'd get excellent references.

She turned back to the two of them. "We need to get out of here."

The two of them shook their heads. "We've tried, there's no way out. We can't find the door or anything else. Food appears periodically by the light, but we aren't sure how." They wore identical, hopeless expressions on their faces. "There is no escape."

Sereen surveyed the room, trying to discern its secrets. "There has to be a way out. Were you awake when I got here?"

"No," They spoke in unison. "We were asleep."

"If there's a way in there's a way out."

They were getting fed, daily. Because neither one of them looked under fed. Despite their advanced appearance they looked healthy. Sereen stopped with that thought. She'd looked horrible, pale and wan, in no way a healthy creature, while these two looked very good for their age. Nyriee had done something different to them than what she'd been doing to her. Some different type of magic. They'd had a spell cast on them, but what had Nyriee done to her? She'd lived with Nyriee her entire life, couldn't remember not living with her. It was possible it was a spell. But she'd never looked old, only tired and grey. Never stooped or turned to a gnarled crone.

She shrugged her off her thoughts. It was most urgent they get out of here. They needed to escape. Now.

***

Kris smiled at his own reflection. Something tried to burst to the fore of his mind, taking away the smile on his face, but he shook it away. There was nothing to interfere with his happiness. Everything was perfect. It had been a bare week since he'd met her, but in that time he'd fallen hard. There had never been such a creature before. Shaking his head more vigorously he tried to dispel the sense of unease he'd been plagued with all day. The feeling he was missing something, but couldn't remember. Thankfully it disappeared when he was around her. Tonight though he was going to make an announcement that would ensure he was always with her.

He straightened his clothing again, brushing away some imagined fuzz here and there. He wanted to be meticulous for her. Everything needed to be right tonight. He'd informed his father of his wishes. Much to his disbelief his father hadn't been as enthused about his announcement as he'd expected.

Since his return his father had been somewhat less than excited about the entire wife hunt. He'd been very recalcitrant about Nyssa, not committing one way or another. It bothered him—something danced just there, out of reach, but he couldn't remember the rest of his thought. His father was worrying him, Nyssa was perfect, but his father seemed unwilling to see that. Sighing he turned away from his reflection, wishing he understood why his father wouldn't see how amazing she was. She would make the perfect Mrs. Claus. With one last check he started out of the room. Time to retrieve his Lady.

***

Nyriee twirled in front of the mirror. Her plan was going off without a hitch. A carefully whispered spell in his ear and he was eating out of her hand. Everything was flawless, tonight he'd declare his love, get down on bended knee and ask her, almost beg her to marry him.

She pursed her painted lips delicately, checking her appearance. She needed to be flawless for her engagement night. The people needed to fall in love with her in this bewitching scene, the same as the Prince. Her smile dimmed at the thought of that old goat St. Nick. He was the hitch in her perfect plan.

Try as she might she couldn't make the fat old Elf to like her, no matter the spell she whispered. He remained impervious to her charms and it appeared there was nothing she could do about it. If the old man had his way she had little doubt that she wouldn't be Kris's chosen bride. Who he thought would be more suitable was beyond her. She'd made sure she was above reproach in her every action and deed. Ensuring that other possible candidates were found lacking, making sure there was a scandal or the like, dirtying them. He could find no fault with her, so why he didn't want her to marry his son was beyond her.

She'd deal with him soon enough. Such reticence would carry over to the people and whatever favor she'd curried among them would die a cruel death if Santa Claus didn't approve of her. He would disappear and die, she'd be merciful though, he'd die quickly and be forevermore with his wife. For his sake she hoped he changed his mind about her. She wouldn't allow anyone to interfere with her plans. The moment the ring was on her finger her plans for him would finish their formation. Already she had several ideas about how to dispose of him.

Placing the finishing touches on her hair she smiled at her reflection, noticing Luce in the mirror.

She whirled, showing her unbridled pleasure in her situation. She soon would have everything she wanted and now she'd be done with him as well. Holding herself imperiously she tried to look down at him, which only made him smile.

"Luce, I've got her contained for you. She's waiting for you to collect her."

His smile was dark, full of some unnamed menace. He pressed a kiss to her cheek. "You look simply ravishing my dear. Youth becomes you."

Her coy laugh was full of that same dark ideal. "You flatter me too much."

"Never." He took a quick look around the room, then looked her up and down. "You have done well for yourself. Tonight's the night?"

"Of course. A week is just long enough to prepare for this magical wedding, it will be held so just as the clock chimes midnight we kiss. It will be magical and entrench me in the people's minds."

"You have it all planned out. I'll stick around for a while, bear witness to this event."

Her smile was an attempt at gentle understanding. Underneath though was ruthless cunning. "Of course I would expect nothing less." She took one last glance at her reflection in the mirror. "It shall be my crowning achievement. The jewel in my crown. Soon everyone will be under my thumb." She cast him a sideways glance. "Except you of course, let me know if there is ought that you need."

"I shall indeed."

Taking a quick glance at the clock she made a shooing motion towards him. "Forgive me, but he shall be here any moment."

He bowed low. "Let me be the first then to give you congratulations." Shadows surrounded him and he vanished.

Chapter Eleven

It had taken some serious magic but she'd found the door. It had been hidden behind some crates and if she hadn't used her magic they never would have found it, or opened it. The door had been sealed with magic as well. It had taken a while to call up enough magic and had resulted in the sweaty exhaustion she was now feeling.

The Palace swayed for a moment as a wave of dizziness assailed her. She was happy to note they weren't too far away, an easy walk, which they did at a run despite her fatigue, everything in her screaming for urgency. Areenie and Floria were in good shape despite their apparent advanced age. In the light they looked less crone like than they had in the shadows. The snow had slowed them some, but not much.

The Palace seemed empty, no visible sign of life. Sereen groaned when they went down yet another hall and found no one. This was getting insane. Someone had to be here. They hadn't just disappeared.

Finally they made their way to the kitchen. It was virtually empty, the only people left were the some very lowly cook's assistants, who were scuttling about, moving as fast as possible. They stood back for several minutes, watching until they slowed for a moment.

"Excuse me. What's going on? Where is everyone?"

The servants stared at her as if she was insane. They were frazzled, but about them was a sense of joy. They all shared a look, as if trying to determine if she was serious or not, then shaking their heads they pushed the youngest of them forward. She looked to the others nervously as if this was some new test they'd just devised to torture her, but they'd returned to work.

"You must've been away for awhile milady," The girl spoke softly and dropped into a low curtsy. Sereen realized with a start she was still wearing the dress and looked like a great Lady and doubted these cook's assistants had any idea as to who she actually was. They thought she was a Lady and therefore couldn't be ignored, otherwise a fit could be thrown, wasting their time.

Instead of correcting their mistake she nodded, "Yes, it's been a while."

The girl nodded, this was something she'd obviously expected. The girl glanced at the other servants then continued. "Well, since the Prince finally returned there's been this Lady that's caught his eye. He's been with her every day and night since. He's positively enamored of her and, well…" She paused with a smile on her face, building the suspense, then leaned in conspiratorially. "Tonight's the night!"

Sereen shook her head, trying to understand, "What do you mean?"

The girl groaned, obviously exasperated by this lack of intelligence. "He's going to ask her to marry him! It's the perfect time too, with a mere week left to the King's ultimatum. Just enough time to plan a wedding!"

Sereen could only stare at the girl in disbelief. What had Kris gone and done? Trying to keep her face cool and composed to make sure the girl didn't guess how she was panicking inside she spoke softly to the girl, she didn't deserve the angst she was feeling over the fact Kris was about to propose to someone—

"Who is K—the Prince, marrying?"

The girl gave her an astounded look. "Why Nyssa of course!"

Only by the greatest strength of will did Sereen keep her mouth from dropping open in horror. Quickly she grabbed her, "When is he proposing?"

"Why now, of course!"

Sereen was gone before the girl finished her sentence. There was only one place where such a proposal would take place.

***

The scene that met her tired eyes when they reached the Great Hall was one out of a nightmare. A pathway was open in the crowd, leading up to the thrones, where St. Nicholas stood looking out across the assembly. Walking up that pathway was Nyssa and Kris.

As she stared down at him from the balcony, Nyssa's hand on his arm her heart broke into more pieces than she thought possible. She'd thought she could let him move on with his life, be a noble person. But looking at him now, she realized she wasn't so cold, couldn't do so without her own heart bursting into a million pieces. Her heart would never be whole after this, no matter how many pieces she managed to put back together, it would always remain a shell of what it had once been.

Areenie and Floria prodded her in the back, urging her on, pushing her until she was down on the floor by the crowd. All she wanted to do was turn back around and run the other way. Their nudging hands kept her moving forward, until she stood at the front of the crowd as Kris and Nyssa turned towards the assembly.

Kris's sweeping gaze landed upon her and his mouth dropped open in horror that turned quickly to revulsion. In that moment she realized the Prince well and truly had broken his promise, he'd forgotten her. And with his forgetting all her hopes were dashed. She turned away from him, burying her face in her hands. Tears welled in her eyes as she started away from him, wanting only to escape the hall as quickly as possible.

There was a loud voice suddenly echoing through the Hall and everything abruptly went black.

Chapter Twelve

Nyriee awoke slowly, unwilling to return to consciousness. Slowly it all flooded back in, bleak and painful, burning through her as she realized what had happened. One moment she'd been starring happily at her soon to be fiancé, gloating at her triumph, the next his face had gone slack with horror as his eyes found *her* in the crowd. It had taken years of practice to keep her reaction from showing through, it had been something dark and horrible. Somehow Sereen had gotten free and had come to ruin her, all of her plans going down the drain as the sight of her broke the spell on the Prince.

Dread filled her as she looked around the room, recognizing it as her personal room in Luce's castle. A room she'd prayed to never again end up in. It was bleak and cold, stark. She'd been tortured and trained unmercifully in this room. Back here she was nothing. Dread filled her and in defiance and anger she screeched like a banshee.

"You idiot! Why steal us, you have the girl! You need us not!" She could hear her voice echoing through the halls.

It seemed the next instant he was there, sitting in the chair, staring down at her calmly where she sat on her knees howling curses.

"I had hoped you would see the stroke of genius in the action, but I can see your ambitions have clouded your judgment." He stood abruptly, glowering over her. "I take recriminations from no one. I have made your way easier. But you," Running his fingers down her cheek, he made her shiver. His hands always like ice. "You need to remember your place Nyriee, and remember it well. You will stay with me until I am done with you and your Prince. Then maybe…" He let the sentence trail off with ugly portent.

He gestured broadly to the room. "This is your room, or your prison, whichever way you choose to look at it."

The door thudded closed, a final note as he left. Nyriee let out a scream of outrage and hurried to it, trying to open it, only to find it immovable, just like always, just like him. "What do you need with me!" Her scream echoed only back to her.

There would be no escape. She had magic, but nothing comparable to Luce's. She was stuck here until he saw fit to release her. Whenever that was. A new darker fear curled around her, what if he planned on releasing her only upon the signing of a new contract?

"No, no." She moaned, "You can't do this to me!" Placing her head in her hands she collapsed back to the ground, rocking back and forth. She'd just escaped, she didn't want to be forced back in again. It had been so perfect, so close. She'd been so near success and he'd taken it from her. Always he loomed over her, reminding her who was Master. Hopefully he would be finished with them all soon. She wanted to return to her plans, but as the walls of her prison closed around her there was only one thought: he would never finish with her.

***

Sereen stared brokenly at the walls of her prison, but couldn't bring herself to care. None of it mattered. Not anymore. He'd gone and fallen for a Witch. The Witch that had held her captive for the entirety of her life. The Witch who would use him, as she'd used her own daughters and destroy him. He'd undoubtedly taken one look at her and fallen head over heels in love.

She had to give Nyriee credit though. Throughout the entirety of her life she'd stood strong, despite everything Nyriee had done to break her, but this had finally done the impossible. Nyriee'd finally found her weak spot, a chink in the armor.

Sobs tore from her throat as she lay there everything inside her felt broken, everything battered.

***

Kris felt like a ton of bricks had been dropped on him and there was no escape from them. He couldn't believe he'd forgotten her, the one thing he'd promised her he wouldn't do he'd done anyway. He'd begged her to trust him and she had, and he'd broken that trust. From the expression on her face he'd broken something else as well.

"Uhgg." Groaning he banged his head against the wall. Cursing himself an idiot. He'd had a treasure beyond compare and he'd thrown her away, for what? Nyssa was a very sweet person, but she couldn't begin to compare. How could he have forgotten? How could he have destroyed something so fragile?

Self recriminations came to the forefront as he thought of the fact he'd been standing there, ready to announce an engagement to Nyssa and hadn't once thought of Sereen.

***

The door to her room creaked open, revealing a supremely handsome man. Through bleary eyes she watched him. A dull thought entered her brain that something was off, but it was quickly dismissed. He walked towards her, a careful cadence to his walk, as one would walk if they were afraid to frighten something or someone that could not wait.

"Forgive me my dear, I've had other matters to attend." His voice was gentle, with a grating quality to it though that rubbed in the wrong way. Sereen couldn't find the will to reply to him, why should she? She didn't care that she was locked in a room. Tired beyond belief she stared up at him, wanting only that he would disappear, leaving her to her misery.

"I can see this has been most rough on you. Come now, I shall give you the hospitality you've been so richly deserving."

Instead of offering his hand he simply reached down and pulled her to her feet. Holding her tightly he placed her hand firmly on his arm, as one would imagine a Lord and Lady. The red dress was one befitting a Lady, and with her looks she appeared to be one, but she didn't feel like one, she felt like a corpse, with nothing left to give life. The dress had long ago passed filthy and she was in desperate need of a bath.

The man led her on a grand tour of the castle showing her many beautiful sights. Her mind was dazed with pain, but even through it the niggling thought something was off remained. There was some quality missing, some inexplicable factor that couldn't be simply placed, it had to be found.

At the end of the tour she was brought into a room with a long table, set with ornate china. She found it overwhelming, but decided to hold her tongue, unwilling to offend. He sat her with a flourish and throughout the meal tried to engage her in meaningless banter. He failed on every count.

She could see the frustration was getting to him, but she couldn't stop, couldn't force herself to care about his feelings on the matter. He'd been polite and nice to her the whole time, despite how disgusting she was. Everything was bland and boring after Kris's betrayal and she found no reason to pretend otherwise. This man—She looked up with a start.

"What's your name?"

Pleasure and energy seemed to suffuse him at this sign of life.

"Forgive, my dear, I am Luce. I simply forgot in all the excitement of finally meeting you to introduce myself. It's been a very long while since the need has arisen." Abashed he turned his face away, "I'm afraid it's been quite some time since I've been in such stunning company and I quite forgot my manners."

Sereen couldn't help, but blush at the compliment. Living with Nyriee there'd been no compliments and even with Kris they'd been lacking. Perhaps she hadn't been beautiful until they returned to the castle. Looking back over the time they'd spent together she had to admit there were obvious signs of his lack of feeling everywhere she looked.

"You're fine, I'm Sereen, by the way."

His smile was full of some wolfish knowledge. "I know, my dear. But please shall we continue?"

She nodded her head lightly, "Of course."

The food was boring despite its richness, but she allowed herself to be drawn into conversation with him. It appeared Luce was quite a person, very kind and considerate, perfect in every way.

***

Over the next several days Sereen got to know Luce. Their days fell into a pattern, he'd send a serving woman to help her dress in lavish finery he'd provided and bring her breakfast. Then she'd spend her mornings doing whatever struck her fancy, in the afternoons he'd appear and they'd spend until the late evening together. Luce was a very compelling and endearing person, and whatever that something was he was missing he more than made up for with everything else.

He was steadfast and solid where Kris had been more wild and unpredictable, something that if she missed now she was sure could be overcome with time, for dealing with Kris would have gotten old in a hurry. Luce would never break her heart, for despite all of his good points there was a piece missing that would induce her to fall in love with him as she had Kris. He could never break her heart, because he could never hold it the way Kris did. Kris had been a storm swallowing her in its tempest, into its wildness, while Luce was a calm lake, allowing her to come at her own pace, allowing her to make the decisions. He was full of patience as he slowly drew her back out of her shell.

Sereen looked up at the moon, almost full, something niggling at the back of her memory about the full moon, but it was nothing she could recall, and it didn't seem that important. Nothing really seemed important here, everything would be fine no matter what happened. It had an ethereal and out of this world quality to it.

Smooth hands reached out and held both her hands as Luce spun her to look at him. "Sereen, I believe the time has come that I speak of my true intentions."

Even before he said them she already knew, could have predicted it down to the last word spoken. She'd known that eventually he would speak, it had simply been a matter of how long he would wait. There was always a motive behind all niceties.

"Yes, Luce, I accept." Was that dreamy voice hers? She couldn't believe herself. Luce it seemed couldn't either, he appeared quite taken aback.

"You know what I'm going to ask?"

Nodding she soothingly rubbed his hands as he held firmly to hers. "Yes, Luce, and as I said I accept."

Instead of giving some indication of his joy he merely nodded. "It shall be done at once then, allow me to escort you back to your rooms."

Sereen inclined her head, a war was going on in her head, and she predicted it would give her a monster headache. Half of her was screaming that she didn't love him and couldn't do this, the other half said she should, it was the right decision to not risk getting hurt again.

It didn't matter, she'd said she would and that was the end. She'd marry Luce and be—be—be content she hoped.

Chapter Thirteen

Luce grinned darkly at Sereen's door. She'd accepted, he hadn't even had to ask. He'd thought his plan was going well, but until she'd accepted he still hadn't been certain, there'd been too much that could have changed her mind. It appeared she'd forgotten all about the Princeling, something he'd been extremely worried about. He'd initially feared he'd have to break her from him, do something drastic. But Nyriee had done her job well.

As he strode down the hall towards the room Nyriee was being held in he couldn't resist the dark laughter bubbling up through him. It had been far too simple. He'd anticipated a fight, a long and difficult journey to win her over, or to at least get her to agree. There had been nothing difficult in it. It had been remarkably easy to turn her, to convince her he was a good man and worthy of her. When he'd asked today he'd been almost afraid he'd asked too soon, that the timing wasn't quite right. Now he'd have her by Christmas.

He had Nyriee to thank for the Christmas Star's acquiescence. If she hadn't managed to befuddle the

Prince into believing she was the innocent Nyssa, deserving of his devotion, and cast a spell to make Sereen drift away from his mind this would have taken longer or maybe not happened. Not that it would have mattered, but the thought was there that he might have had to harm the Prince. Now he'd have Nyriee control the Prince and he'd control Nyriee. The puppets would all be in their proper places. Nyriee would think she was free, but would still bow to the puppet master's strings, strings she wouldn't notice.

It wasn't long before he stood before Nyriee's door. He hadn't been to see her since her first day back, choosing to allow her to stew on her actions and how easily he could reduce her to nothing but a slave again.

Instead of knocking he walked in. She was sitting on the only chair in the room that sat facing the window, staring blankly into the night. Not turning towards him or giving him the respect he so justly deserved she spoke.

"It's a beautiful night, isn't it Luce?" She paused as creatures moved in the shadows. "I saw you earlier with her, has she obliged you yet? Do you have your heart's desire?"

"Not yet, but she has agreed. Now it is time for you to take the Prince and leave."

Nyriee finally looked at him, her eyes were icy, but her tone conveyed none of what could be going on in that head of hers. "Only a matter of time then. What did it take Luce? What was the catalyst? Hmm?"

"The Prince was the catalyst, as I'd already expected. But you, Nyriee, are the reason she agreed. The Prince fell in love with you and broke her poor heart, now in retaliation she's chosen me."

She nodded and turned away, "Yes, that would fit. What if the Prince no longer wants to be with me?"

Luce shook his head at her, "I'm sure Nyssa can convince him that he loves her and induce him to leave with her."

She licked at her lips, a purely unplanned action. "What if I can't Luce, what if I don't want to?"

Before she could move his hand was around her throat, fury pumping hot and hard through his blood. "Then make him. You did it once, you will do it again."

"Ahhg." Nyriee yelped as Luce threw her away from him. She landed on her side, barely saving herself from hitting her head.

"You are wise Nyriee, I'm sure you'll be able to figure it out. Now go, before I decide you don't deserve the gift I'm giving." He pointed toward the door, the desire to place her more firmly where she belonged a steady thrum in his ears. Keeping her head low she slunk out the door, refusing to make eye contact with the monster.

***

Nyriee walked blindly, blinded by fury such as she had never felt. Luce treated her as if she was dirt, even after what she'd done for him. She'd get him, somehow she'd get him. Now though she needed to get herself and the Prince out of here before Luce changed his mind and went off the deep end.

From memory she found the Prince's cell. Luce had placed the Prince in a real cell, probably to make a point. It unnerved her to see him in a cell like the lowest peasant. Shaking her head she pulled herself together. Time to make an entrance such as to ensure he suspected nothing of how she'd arrived or managed to get him out.

Dawn was just peeking as she placed her hand on the door.

***

Kris glanced out the window into the dark day before him. He couldn't remember how long he'd been trapped in the cell, sometimes it seemed like days, others years. He'd lost track of all time. He slept when exhaustion overcame him, but mostly he stared out the barred window, wishing his actions away. He'd caught his reflection in the window the day after last and what he'd seen wasn't promising. He was covered in filth from head to toe and looked gaunt and worn. Nothing like the Prince of Christmas Land should. It didn't matter though, nothing mattered. He'd broken Sereen's heart, and now he was stuck here and could do nothing about it.

But he couldn't take it back and tell her he loved her, had fallen in love with her before she was beautiful, before everything. The very first moment he'd met her face to face scared to death, the moment she'd stood up to him. And he wished he could take everything back.

He looked up with a start when the door banged into the wall. And stared blankly at Nyssa as she burst into his cell.

"Oh, Kris! You're alright." She fell into him, clinging as if afraid he would disappear. "I was so afraid."

Clutching her close he stared down at her. So good, so sweet and deserving. Looking down in her eyes brimming with tears he asked her softly, the question that had been part of his torture.

"Nyssa, do you love me?"

***

Nyriee froze, a wash of emotions flooding through her. Did she love him? She opened her mouth to speak, only to snap it closed again. All she had to do was say the words, he was a good person, if she claimed to love him he wouldn't break her heart, but something held her back.

She loved his money, his power, the aura that would surround being his wife, but she knew that she didn't love him. Love had never been a factor in the equation, not on her end. The point had always been to make him fall in love with her, not the other way around.

Once again she opened her mouth and started to say the words that would give her all of those things she'd craved. Except—Sereen, tears running down her face as she stared down at them, Kris's broken features, Sereen giving her the life she'd always dreamed of, and finally Luce, laughing as he told her he would marry the Christmas Star, posses her for all eternity.

All of those images running through her mind she opened her mouth and told him the absolute truth, something she couldn't remember doing in years.

"No, Kris, I don't love you."

Kris froze at her words and looked at her wildly. He looked shocked and sick to his stomach.

Nyriee on the other hand felt as light as a butterfly. She wanted to jump up and down with joy, it was the most honest thing she'd done in her life and it felt great. Before he could stop her she twirled out of his grasp and gave a couple of spins, much as she'd seen her daughters do several times, coming to a stop directly in front of him. Grasping his hands she shook them up and down, while dancing in front of him.

"Oh, Kris." His mouth was gaping open as he stared at her astonishment, something about his open mouth, reminded her about Sereen. "Oh, Kris, we've got to go!"

Hurrying over to the door she grabbed the handle, unsurprised to find it solid and unmoving. For a second she stared at it then poured magic into it along with a careful chant and voila, the door burst open. She gave herself a self-satisfied smile. He thought he could contain her with such entry level magic? She'd show him! Holding tightly to Kris, who seemed to have recovered only slightly they made a mad dash down the halls running for all they were worth towards the Great Hall. Time to ensure that Luce didn't take possession of the Christmas Star.

***

Strong hands helped Sereen dress in a gown of shimmering green. Not a dress she would have chosen for herself with its low cut and clingy material, delineating every curve and plane. The woman helping her was very efficient, moving with quick sure movements, like she'd dressed people for their weddings many a-time. Sereen simply stood under her treatment, neither helping or hindering. What did anything matter? The dress didn't matter, the event she was about to take part in didn't matter, the woman in front of her didn't matter.

As the final touches went on her hair she glanced in the mirror, cocking her head to the side as she looked at the woman next to her.

The woman had dull grey, frizzing hair, but it must have been a beautiful shimmering white at one point. Her skin was a milky white, the strange thing though were her eyes, so deep blue, like the sky fading into night. Sereen laughed internally at her own whimsy, something tickling the back of her mind, something that it didn't want to forget.

Tired she shook her, head forcing herself to try to forget. It didn't matter now, no memory was going to change the fact she was getting married to a man that seemed to be missing something vital. With a vigorous shake of her head she took notice again of the woman in the mirror. There was something about her... Those eyes seemed so familiar. Those eyes should have been laughing, dancing, there should be no lines bracketing the woman's mouth except those of laughter.

Wrinkling her brow in consternation she reached out and touched the woman, all of her confusion and desire to see the woman as she should look pouring through the touch.

She startled when the woman gasped, what had she said her name was? Holly? It didn't matter she was setting Kris free from her heart and marrying this other creature. She half turned when the woman didn't retake her ministrations.

The woman was no longer there.

In her place was a visage that was both beautiful and lively. Silver hair, sparkling blue eyes, the woman was a little on the plump side, just as she should be. Sereen smiled at the thought, now she was right, now she was perfect. The woman stared at her in wonder, mouth gaping open, those eyes danced anyway though, what did they care of shock?

"I thought I would never live to see this day, Christmas Star." The woman dropped a perfect, low curtsy, while Sereen stared at her confused.

"What are you talking about?"

Dismay crossed the woman's features. "You're the Christmas Star, the soul so pure that the Christmas Star chose you to bear her power. You light up the galaxy despite your small size. The one that led the Three Wise Men to Bethlehem where Christ the Lord lay in the manger. You lit the way. It touched you, making you part of it, part of it that lit the way."

"No, that's not—I'm sorry you're thinking of—someone else."

The woman shook her head, "No I'm certain Christmas Star, Sereen. You are she, one of the Star Touched, most powerful of the Star Touched."

It was too much to wrap her head around and in an attempt to distract herself she asked the first question that popped into her head. "Who are you?"

"Oh, why I'm Holly Claus." Absolute seriousness reflected on her face.

Sereen stared at her, astounded. "The Holly Claus?"

Holly nodded, "Yes, I am she."

"But you're dead."

Holly looked taken aback. "What do you mean dead?"

"Dead, everyone thinks you died over one hundred and twenty years ago. Everyone thinks you're dead."

Tears filled Holly's eyes, eyes she recognized now that she really looked, they were Kris's eyes, same laughing tilt and mischievous glint in them, never knowing what plans lay behind them. Now Sereen knew where Kris got them his nature from.

"Even Kris… and Nick?" Holly got out brokenly.

Tears clogged Sereen's throat as she nodded, unable to form words. Holly's pain was real and not to be taken lightly. She sat down on the bed with little aplomb.

"So long… All this time I didn't remember. How could I have forgotten those I loved?" She cried.

Sereen stared at Holly Claus, a nasty feeling spreading through her, flooding her blood with ice. What was Holly doing here? "What do you mean you forgot?"

Holly shook her head, regretful sobs bursting forth. "I just—I just couldn't remember. There was nothing there."

Sereen knelt next to Holly, wrapping her arms around her, offering comfort to a woman broken by what she couldn't control. Sereen's own tears added to the puddle, tears for her own stupidity. What if Kris had simply forgotten because of a spell, like Holly, and she'd just thrown him away acting as judge, jury, and executioner?

Tears of remorse and shame rolled down her cheeks. As she cried them out a new steel formed in her spine, she was getting out of here. Now. And she was taking Holly with her. She'd go beg Kris to forgive her if necessary. Something wasn't right, she couldn't go through with marrying Luce. Whatever was wrong with Luce, he'd known about Holly, had probably done this to her.

"Come on Holly, we're getting out of here. Now."

She pulled her towards the door.

***

The castle was a maze of icy passages. Once the spell had been broken over Holly it seemed she couldn't remember directions, some part of the spell had always told her were to go. Sereen groaned when they rounded yet another corner, seeming no nearer an exit. Holly had remembered that the way out was somewhere along the Great Hall, so now they were frantically searching. Only they weren't getting any closer to the Hall. Every turn seemed to be taking them further away from where they wanted to go. The first time they'd taken a wrong turn they'd attempted to break a window, it hadn't worked. In the process they'd found the windows were spelled. The entire castle was probably spelled to keep Luce's prey in.

After several more turns with no luck, she pulled Holly to a stop and reached for the magic. Slowly she grasped hold of it and sent it out, looking for the path out as she'd done in the basement. It was faint at first, so much so that she had to use more magic, hunting.

They'd been going the wrong way the entire time. Tugging on Holly she moved back along the way they'd come.

Agitation and an irrational fear was taking her over. It was difficult to hold onto the magic, it was taking so much, rapidly draining her. Fear was taking hold now that something was draining her, something that didn't want her getting out. Swallowing the acrid taste in her mouth she continued on, even as the quivering in her stomach got worse. Every step towards the Hall was an effort. Finally they burst into the Hall, and were brought to an abrupt stop.

Luce sat on an iron throne that overlooked the entire Hall, wrought with horrible images. He slouched in it, carelessly. She realized that she hadn't been in this terrible room before.

The walls were covered in depictions of horrible things. Black and blood red it looked like a scene out of a horrible nightmare. The walls of the corridors had been constant crimson as they'd rushed past them she remembered, as had all the others, but she'd never taken true notice of it before. This was an area of the castle she'd never seen before and now she realized why, this was who he was and she'd never have agreed to marry this creature.

Stuck on the floor as if glued there were Nyriee and Kris. It pulled Sereen up short and served only to increase the fluttery feeling in her stomach. Panic filled her as Luce lowered his gaze to them, as if they were ants, here, but below his notice.

"Kind of you to join Sereen, and you brought Holly with you, very clever."

All of the excuses and reasons she could come up with swirled in her mind, none of them seemed possible, all of them incoherent. She'd cut off the power the moment they'd entered the hall. Luce had undoubtedly been feeling the power emanating from her though

Something needed to be said and finally in a choked voice she managed to get something out. "Luce, I didn't expect to find you here."

His laugh rolled dark and deep through the hall, causing shivers of dread to chase down her spine. A whole flock of butterflies had taken up residence in her stomach and they were doing the rumba. She was certain she looked green and about ready to fall over. When he finally stopped the look in his eyes was something not of this world, or any other.

"Of course you didn't, my dear."

The words she'd been about to say stuck in her throat as she stared at him. Pure undaunted horror engulfed her as he rose and walked to her.

"It is a rare occasion when these halls host such a beauty as you." His smile was dark, glowing with a menace beyond her ken.

"Tha—thank you." Mentally she cursed herself, she was doing a great job of appearing weak before him. She couldn't see Kris anymore, only Luce, who loomed large and filled her vision. She tried to peer around him and he noticed the path of her gaze. He half turned, looking towards Kris, but keeping her in his sights. "Ahh, the Prince. Is that why you came? To find him?"

Any answer would have an ill effect she felt and it was imperative that she get Kris, Holly, and—Nyriee, as much as it hurt, out of here. Her gaze met Kris's across the room, in it she could read his worry, angst, and regret. Slowly she raised her eyes to Luce. Tilting her head to the side, she did the best impression of a Lady she could manage.

"I came to find you," Ignoring every sense of self-preservation coursing through her she laid her hand lightly on Luce's shoulder. "I believe you spoke of a ceremony we were to complete today." Sultry and low, her voice came across as one of a seductress and seemed to appease him, at least his terrible look disappeared. "Yes, indeed, come you're friends can watch." He held out his arm and restraining the shuddering she felt burning through her body she accepted it.

"They were just on their way out, but I thought they could wait and see this deed done, to its fullest extent."

Sereen smiled as best she could, though it felt tight and fake, even to her, hopefully he wouldn't notice. Their best bet would be if she could get him to relax and zap him somehow, then they all could make a break for it. She'd deal with Nyriee and Kris once they were all out. By the expression on Nyriee's face Luce scared her something fierce, to leave her behind would be an act of unparalleled cruelty.

Taking deep breaths she calmed her panicky heart and tried to appear at ease and unaffected by the world around her. He relaxed subtly as the seconds passed, it was barely noticeable, but she had to pay attention. She'd been trying to leave her magic sleeping since they'd entered the hall, waiting for the proper moment and trying to keep him from becoming suspicious.

"The deed will be done shortly my dear, worry not."

She breathed out gustily, "I should hope so." He'd obviously noticed her nerves, but had mistaken it for something it wasn't. Luce turned his back to her, reaching for something, and she struck.

Reaching out she pressed her hand to his back, as if steadying him and reached for her core. Her intent was not to harm, only to knock him out for long enough to get away. He dropped with a solid thud to the ground. Shakily she released the breath she'd been holding in and backed away from his fallen body. Holly's hands were on her shoulders for a moment then they were hurrying towards Kris and Nyriee.

Luce's unconsciousness had released the bonds that had held them in place.

"Come on we need to go." As she turned to go Kris's hand landed heavily on her shoulder, turning she met his deep blue eyes. "Kris, we need to go."

He shook his head, holding her in place. "Sereen, I can't begin to tell you how sorry I am—"

Sereen looked wildly to where Luce lay, tugging at his hand she spoke in a rush, "It doesn't matter now, we've got to go, come on!"

With his other hand he grasped her chin and tilted her face up towards his. "It does matter, I broke my promise, and I hurt you, a lot. You didn't deserve that. I can't—"

Laughter echoed throughout the hall as Luce awoke.

Chapter Fourteen

It was too late.

Any chance they'd held of escaping had disappeared when Luce awoke, there would be no other opportunities.

Sereen closed her eyes, trying to calm the race of fear beating like a drum through her blood.

"Very clever my dear, but just as I underestimated you, you've underestimated me." He grinned at her venomously, blood on his teeth. "You'll have to kill to incapacitate me enough to escape. You might as well accept you have no choice, come let this be over with." The implied threat was clear: if you don't, prepare to have those around you destroyed. The world wouldn't be right without Kris.

Luce's hand was outstretched grasping, reaching, for her, hunger shining in his eyes. Reluctantly she moved to place her hand in his, aware of Kris's eyes boring into her. Almost—

"STOP!" Kris's voice reverberated through the hall, echoing with despair and anger. He grabbed her, pulling her away from Luce, tugging her roughly into his grasp. As he spun her she had a disconcerting view of the hall before she came face to face with him.

"What *are* you doing?" She glared at him darkly, if she did this he could escape, leave and be safe.

"I can't allow you to do this, you don't want to do this." His eyes burned with a fierce passion that she'd only glimpsed briefly before, his voice fraught with ominous peril.

As she stared at him she realized she would do whatever it took to ensure his survival. "Kris, let me go, I want to do this." Silently she pleaded with him, begging him to understand. Instead acquiescing he shook his head.

"I can't let you," Instead of forcing her to see his point he grabbed her and started to drag her away. Luce watched the entire interlude with a smile on his face, but as she was pulled along after Kris his expression started to change, dark fury starting to form.

"Kris, you need to stop."

Every fiber in her being tightened before it happened. Hairs stood at attention, as she turned to stop it, to draw on the magic—

The blast knocked her off her feet and away from Kris.

She landed hard on the unyielding stone, Kris was on the opposite end of the hall, unmoving. Footsteps sounded in the hall as Areenie and Floria came running. They stopped dead at the scene being played out.

All the while Luce was looming closer. Revulsion filled her as she stared at his looming form, everything in her screaming to get away from him.

When Areenie and Floria appeared she took the opportunity, to check on Kris.

"WHERE DO YOU THINK YOU'RE GOING?" His voice reverberated off the walls of the Hall, making it louder and more threatening. Suddenly something was holding her, keeping her from moving. He'd used his magic on her, and try as she might she couldn't break it.

"You just couldn't do the reasonable thing, you had to go the hard way, you had to listen to that—" He gestured in Kris's direction.

Sereen shook her head, "Please, don't."

Luce sneered at her. "That incident at the cottage just didn't do the job did it? It was supposed to remove the Princeling, and lead you straight into my arms, everything has always been to lead you into my arms!"

Sereen swallowed with difficulty as she stared at him. He'd expanded with rage and appeared as a dark visage from a nightmare, her worst nightmare. His hands turned to claws, black wings on his back, skin and eyes gone red.

"The night Nyriee told me of your whereabouts I knew I had to come up with a plan. Those parents of yours were too nice, too loving, they'd train you in your powers." He smiled evilly at her, "So I removed them, the only fault was that somehow they managed to send you to Nyriee, tying her to you as your guardian." Stopping he sneered at Nyriee who was standing quivering by the wall, clutching it like a lifeline. "Only then did I realize the brilliance of their move, I'd leave you there, allow you to grow under her clutches. She knew nothing of your worth and wouldn't curry what favor she could with you, she'd be cruel and hard."

His ugly, gnarled hand reached out and stroked down Nyriee's cheek, causing her to gasp for breath, as if there was no air left in her lungs. "She fulfilled her part even better than expected, except," His hand tightened around Nyriee's throat and Sereen stood horrified, staring at the pair. "She took you to the Palace, just as she was supposed to be turning you over to my tender care. There you met the Prince, and fell in love. Such a brilliant way to ruin my plans." His lips curled back in distaste.

Sereen barely tamped down the urge to turn towards Kris, to check visually on him. She'd been sending an undercurrent of power towards him throughout Luce's entire speech, trying to keep him as alive and awake as she could from this distance. It was severely tapping her reserves, already she was feeling dizzy and woozy. Since she hadn't been able to break Luce's hold, all she could do was stand there.

Clutching Nyriee's daughters close was Holly, who's eyes continuously darted towards her son. Whatever he'd done had Holly stuck as well, she couldn't move, despite several attempts. She jerked herself back to attention when she realized Luce was still talking.

"And then I decided to simply remove the Prince, except you wouldn't allow him to die, and nearly got yourself killed in the process. Once you returned to court I thought I had you safely tucked away and the Prince would have broken your heart badly enough that you'd place all thought of him out of your mind. Ahh," He smiled, it reminded of her a paternal smile of pride, except sick and twisted in an unnatural way. "But you'd become more in tune with your powers than I thought, I underestimated you, my dear. You recognized Nyriee, even in her disguise, and you escaped, coming to the rescue."

He gestured broadly to the hall, having released his strangle hold on Nyriee who collapsed, gasping, to the floor. "Then I thought I'd found a pressure spot, for you believed that he loved Nyriee, but you loved him enough to do anything for him. Except, again, you saw something you shouldn't have in Holly and came to his rescue. But now my dear, my underestimation of you is done."

Moving so fast she barely saw him, he held Kris in a death grip. Crying out she moved towards them, only to be brought up short by her feet stuck to the ground again, having broken the spell for a second. Panic seized her as she watched blood pour from Kris's multiple wounds inflicted from the blast of magic. Tears streamed down her face as she fell to her knees, trying to scrabble closer, wanting to reach him and not having the strength or power. Luce cackled maniacally at her pain, swinging Kris in such a way that brought a moan to his lips despite his mostly unconscious state.

"STOP! Please, just stop." Her voice broke as she screamed out in anguish, sobs tore from her as she clawed helplessly at the floor, trying to get closer. She didn't notice as her fingers turned bloody or as her voice went hoarse, her only desire to reach Kris, to save him from the monster that held him in his grip.

The demon grinned down at her, taking sick pleasure at her pain. "All you have to do is agree, my dear, say yes." He crooned to her. She watched revolted as he stroked hands turned to red claws down Kris's cheek, leaving black trails. "Just agree, it will be all over, lover boy can go home safe and sound."

She shook her head. Continuing her scrabbling. "Stop, please God, just stop." She whispered, crossing her arms across her chest and rocking back and forth unable to move forward. "Just stop." Everything inside her was broken, nothing mattered except getting Kris free.

She blinked shocked for several minutes when Kris's eyes opened and he stared at her, a crooked smile appearing on his mouth, marred by the blood trickling from his lip.

"Please, just stop." She pleaded desperately, she couldn't take any more of this. It was too much. She'd give anything for him, anything at all. In that second she decided and opened her mouth. Kris seemed to read the intent in her eyes,

"Sereen, don't fall—"

Kris didn't finish his sentence as suddenly Luce placed both his hands on Kris. Dark white light in his hands.

"NO!"

Her scream echoed through the hall as Luce threw Kris's now limp body away from him. Laughter spilling from his lips. She howled like a wild woman when he remained limp, unmoving, as if a corpse. Off in the background was Nyriee, pale with shock, and Holly with the daughters, tears streaming down their faces as they could do nothing.

She looked up bleakly at Luce as he stood over her. Her throat was on fire, her eyes burned, shattered she stared up at Luce as he stared down at her, a soft, twisted smile playing at his lips.

"Let me take all of this away from you, my dear."

In that instant her heart iced over. Everything that she was suddenly turned cold as she looked into his eyes. Reaching up she accepted his proffered hand. He helped her to her feet, steadying her as she stood there reeling. She brought her bloody hands to his shoulders, accepting his touch on her waist. It seemed right, the blood.

Perhaps he read the intent in her eyes, or maybe he already knew. His eyes widened as he opened his mouth, but it was already too late.

Sereen drew all of her power from the very core of her being and poured it into Luce. More power than she'd thought possible. His mouth opened in a silent scream as his eyes bored into her suddenly icy ones. A deep chill purveyed her as she stared at him. Seconds later flames licked around her hands as his skin turned black and curled.

Seconds later, breathing heavily she let him drop to the ground. She felt cold, so cold, without real thought or intent she walked over to Kris and dropped to her knees next to him, rolling him over.

Blood trickled from the corner of his mouth. Battered and bloody he lay on the floor, looking like the victim of an earth war. No tears pricked her eyes, no keening cries from her mouth. Pure purpose filled her as she placed both her hands over his heart. She poured all of her heart and soul into him, wanting only to see his blue eyes one more time.

It didn't matter how long it took, or what it took, she poured all the power from her very being into him. The very fabric of what she was. She could feel the flames licking her own skin, a fire burning through her body, burning away the ice that covered her. It was so hot, leaving nothing in its wake. As the fires burned through her mind and slowly everything flickered in and out of focus, as she felt her very being drift away from what and who she was, those stunning, brilliant blue eyes opened.

A smile lit her mouth, one of pure joy and happiness. She felt his chest rise and fall with a breath. Sereen the Christmas Star poured the very last of what she was into him, giving everything to him, and accepted the darkness that suddenly blanketed her mind. Peace enveloped her, he would live.

Chapter Fifteen

Kris felt tears pouring down his face, a broken sound akin to a howl echoing from his throat as he rocked the lifeless body in his arms. Everything inside felt shattered as he held her to him. She wasn't breathing and there wasn't a thing he could do about it. The blackened body of Luce lay not far, his mother, Nyriee, not Nyssa as she'd told him on their run, and her daughters stood huddled together, clutching each other. Watching him as if afraid he might attack at any time. All he could think, running through his mind in an unending loop was: "She is gone."

Everything was dark. She'd been the light that had made everything else visible, without her there was nothing. And there was nothing he could do. He cradled her close to his chest, tears streaming into her red hair. Everything he was, gone. He wished she'd let him, die, instead he was stuck here while she was gone. For an instant he wished Luce was still alive so he could beg to be sent with her, no one left would have mercy on him, no one left would have pity and kill him. He'd have to figure out how to do it on his own.

***

Slowly around him sparkles appeared. Glittering and shimmering in the brightly lit Hall of evil. He took only the faintest of notice of them, they mattered not. Nothing mattered.

"She would not appreciate your thoughts of death after giving her own life to save yours, Prince."

Blurry eyes looked up at the Queen of the Snowflake Fairies Christabel and Berry, Queen of the Sugar Plum Fairies. There was some protocol for being in their presence, but he cared not about it, hopefully they'd take umbrage and kill him for his insult. He waited hopefully for a moment, only to have it snuffed out when they merely shook their heads at him.

"Little Prince, give her to us. There is naught you can do for her, she has passed beyond this world." Christabel's voice was rich like many voices laid together to form a brilliant tapestry, but Kris could only bring forth the most disconnected appreciation. It didn't matter how beautiful they were, the light was gone, everything was gray and dull now.

Tears continued to roll down his cheeks as the Fairies shook their heads at him. "Oh, little Prince, you are broken because of your loss, and that simply will not do."

When their words registered, he recoiled from their hands, terrified they might attempt to take his thoughts, his pain away.

They did nothing of the sort, instead they seemed to share his pain, and with it understand how destroyed he felt.

Kris looked up, shocked, when two perfect tears landed amongst his on Sereen's cheeks. Fairies didn't cry, but these two, the noblest and proudest of Queens bowed their heads and shared in his agony. Both lightly touched his shoulders than stepped back from him.

He continued to stare down at Sereen's face, wanting to make sure he memorized every plane and angle. If he tried he could pretend she was just sleeping and would wake up soon, being just as she always was. Gah, he wanted her back so bad, his throat felt tight with the pain roaring through it. He was blind to everything but her, couldn't even see the blood that covered her.

He could almost feel her breathing, see her eyelashes fluttering—

"Take good care of her, Prince."

He was so shocked he almost dropped her when he realized her eyelashes were fluttering and she was breathing. Horrified by his almost act, he clutched her tighter, than remembered that she needed to breath and loosened his grip. Her eyelids fluttered one more time and opened, revealing those perfect purple eyes.

Her hands crusted with her own blood reached up and smoothed an errant curl away from his face. Before she could utter a single word he crushed her to him and buried his head in her shoulder.

She combed her fingers through his hair as she held him just as tight. "I love you Kris."

He pulled back, staring at her through blurry eyes. "I'm not worthy of you! You deserve someone as wonderful as you are, not me, a jerk who's never done anything worthwhile in his life."

With gentle hands she cupped his face. "Kris," She breathed softly. "I don't want someone more worthy of me if it means I can't be with you. I love you."

He stared at her, his mouth gaping open. Tenderly she pushed his jaw closed.

"But-that's why-how-?"

She smiled at him softly, "I don't know why or how, but it's the way it is."

Tugging his head down, she pressed her lips to his.

***

The Fairy Queens watched with identical smiles on their faces as the couple embraced. After a moment they separated and two curious faces turned towards theirs. Smiling down at the pair was no task as they looked upon them.

"You must have many questions—"

The pair nodded, but remained holding each other, as if the world would end should they let go.

"But seeing as how it is so close to Christmas we must return the two of you to the Palace." Berry intoned.

Sereen took a look at the Prince then spoke in a tone brooking no refusal. "We have one question, beyond all others your graces, what did Luce want with me?"

Berry and Christabel shared a long look with each other, "We have a moment,"

Berry gave Christabel a stern look, "But only a moment."

With a smile brilliant enough to light the darkest corner Christabel turned towards the pair. "Long ago Luce was an angel of sorts, but he became jealous of power that he had no ability or right to have. In his anger

Luce tried to capture the son of God and present him to Lucifer, but he failed, on all accounts. Everything he did to prevent his birth and his initial rising was thwarted due to the Star that chose you, and thus by you."

Cocking her head to the side Sereen stared at Christabel, puzzlement showing on her face. "Me?"

Both Berry and Christabel nodded their heads. "Yes, you. For you the Christmas Star chose and it lit the way to Bethlehem and for all those that would come to see *him*. In his fury and lust for power Luce tried to steal the true Star from the sky, *you*, from the sky, but he failed even in this. In his failure and attempt at the son of God he fell in Christmas Land, and here vowed to capture its mortal form, for only this would allow him to return to the mortal realm and there take it over, to rule in glory."

Christabel turned towards Berry, "But he couldn't overcome a love you'd found on your own."

Berry giggled softly, a sound one would never expect from such a figure of esteemed royalty. "He thought he could hide you away, keep you from the outside world and force you to him. But you proved him wrong. In underestimating you he misjudged the lengths one would be willing to go to save the one they love."

Kris squeezed Sereen lightly and spoke in a voice chalk full of emotion. "Could you take us back? I'm ready to be home."

The Queens nodded. "Indeed."

Epilogue

The hall was decked in red and green, here and there silver and gold winked at you with its shining luster. Giant swathes of holly and wreathes the sizes of carriage wheels adorned the hall in natural color. Everything was polished to gleam and many of the murals one could almost believe were alive. It teamed with life as the many attendants of the wedding stood chatting or dancing. Soon it would be time to send Saint Nick off on his annual journey through the skies, this year with Mrs. Claus by his side for the first time in years.

Sereen smiled warmly at one of the Ladies that had come to the Palace in an attempt to win the Prince's interest, a Prince who had stood with her at the altar and declared for all to hear that he would love her for all of eternity and beyond. Strangely none of them seemed to bear her any ill will, but with all of the shocking events they were probably too startled to react with anything other than stunned acceptance.

Everything was overwhelming, even to her, and she'd known every nuance. Holly'd been stunning, helping extensively despite her ordeal. Wanting only to throw herself back into all of the life she'd missed.

The wedding was a combination of announcement of Holly's return and a celebration for the beloved Prince's marriage. Despite her urging she'd been unable to persuade Kris to delay the wedding, seeing no reason to rush the wedding with everything that had gone on. But Kris had wanted to fulfill all of his father's requirements and had insisted they tie the knot. He'd also cited some unreasonable fear about other men trying to steal her, which she'd thought silly, and still did. Though she freely admitted that every time she looked in the mirror there was quite a ravishing beauty that stared back.

All of the staff had been exemplary, pulling together everything on such short notice. They'd seemed truly exited once the initial shock had worn off and had thrown themselves in the project with gusto. Many of the plans had already been lain and preparations initiated, but they'd been placed on hold following the Prince's stunning disappearance and they certainly hadn't planned on him wanting to hold the wedding immediately upon his return, they figured he'd want to find an excuse to escape. However they'd managed to do it everything was resplendent. Nothing felt forced or rushed, thrown together on a hair's breadth notice.

Somehow, she wasn't sure how many Elves had been pulled out of toy making, they'd gotten a dress made that was every bride's dream. It was so white it held a tinge of blue and wasn't overly large. Flowing and rippling around her it was reminiscent of a waterfall. Excellent for dancing with just a bit of a train. Like everything else in this fairy tale wedding it was perfect.

Nyriee and her daughters had been released to return to their house. No one saw fit to punish them after all they had suffered. It seemed Nyriee had turned over a new leaf, though only time would tell. No one yet knew if she'd be able to reverse the spell she'd cast on herself and her daughters. Sereen had tried with little avail to reverse it, so now they were hoping Nyriee would find something at her home.

Hoping to add to her turning over her new leaf they'd offered to let her and her daughters come to the wedding, but they'd all refused. They wanted to get started home and hopefully on their way to reversing the spell.

The only question left was what had happened to Sereen's Elfin parents, but no one knew, not even Nyriee, who'd been shocked when Sereen'd shown up at her door. The best guess was that Luce had done something to them, though what who knew. Despite the sadness that plagued her that her parents hadn't been here for her happy day she was enjoying herself. Having Kris's love certainly helped.

Warm hands encompassed her waist as Kris came up behind her.

"They're ready to take off." His breath tickled her ear as he spoke. She nodded and allowed him to lead him off to where Santa's sleigh was ready for takeoff. Hugs and kisses were given out as Santa went off on his yearly trip through the skies with Mrs. Claus at his side to spread merry cheer through the night.

They shared a smile as they watched the sleigh rise. They too were off on the adventure of a lifetime.

The End

Glossary and Pronunciation

Pronunciations are in [ ]

Allisone [Alice-own]—A maid in the Christmas Palace. She often attracts the much desired attentions of the Prince.

Areenie Dantaan [Are-eee-knee]—Youngest daughter of Nyriee. Prettier than her older sister she wants nothing more than to be like her mother.

Berry—Queen of the Sugarplum Fairies. Has black hair with purple highlights and always dresses in maroon. She is the kindest of the pair.

Christabel—Queen of the Snowflake Fairies. Pale as new fallen snow, she appears as if she could disappear into the snows.

Christmas Land—The land where Santa Claus and all those that make Christmas so special live, waiting every year for that special time of year when Santa takes off on his sleigh.

Christmas Star—The Star that rose over the stable where Jesus lay in his manger. It led the three wise men to him. It is the most powerful of the Stars, particularly around Christmas.

Christmas Town—The capital of Christmas Land, it is where Santa's Christmas Palace is. Here Christmas is always just around the corner.

Dantaan [Daan-n-taah-n]—Nyriee married into the family of Dantaan and gave her husband two daughters, Floria and Areenie. They are all that is left of this once noble house.

Elfen [Elf-inn]—The semi-immortal creatures of Christmas Land, neither Elves or Fairies Seren and Nyriee are members of this race. Some of them have magic.

Elves—Shorter in stature typically than Elfen. They help Santa create toys for all the good girls and boys. They all possess some kind of magic. Not all help Santa however, some live simple live simple lives as famers or shopkeepers.

Fairies—These mysterious beings are magical and help spread Christmas joy throughout the mortal earth and Christmas Land.

Floria Dantaan [Floor-Ĭ-aaa]—Oldest daughter of Nyriee, comelier than her sister, but the most levelheaded.

Holly Kringle Claus—Santa Claus's Elfen wife turned immortal. Years ago a terrible accident befell her, taking her life. Santa has mourned for her ever since and Kris has gotten progressively more irresponsible.

King and Queen of Christmas Land—The rulers of Christmas Land, it has been Santa and Holly Claus for as long as Christmas Land has existed. Since Holly Claus's death there has yet to be a new Queen of Christmas Land.

Kristopher Kringle Claus [Christopher]—Son of Santa Claus, also known as Saint Nicholas. He is a scapegrace who has difficulties being responsible.

Lady Nyriee Dantaan [Nigh-ree]—Mother of Areenie and Floria. She is a born Witch and under the control of Luce. She is trying to escape from under his thumb, with little success.

Lady Nyssa [Niece]—The remade version of Nyriee with her full beauty intact. She is stunning and seemingly the perfect wife for the Prince.

Luce [Loose]—An angel fallen from heaven for helping Satan himself. In his attempt to steal the Christmas Star from the sky he was out.

Madame Lacrofft—The Christmas Palace's head seamstress. She is a nice, but lately overworked woman. She can't deal with everyone's demands.

Miriam—The Innkeeper's wife, she is a kindly woman, even if she can be a tad oblivious.

Slate—The sneaking son of Miriam and the Innkeeper. He schemes to get his unsavory hands on Sereen. Not everything is as it seems with him.

Saint Nicholas—King of Christmas Land father of Kristopher Claus. He lost his wife over a hundred years ago in a terrible accident, he still mourns for her.

Santa Claus—See Saint Nicholas.

Sereen [Serene]—The heroin of our tale. She's never known her parents and is an orphan as far as we know. She has lived with Nyriee for as long as she can remember. She is one of the Star Touched.

Star Touched—Those Elfen that are touched by a Star when the Star decides it wishes to share its powers with those below. They end up with some or most of that Star's powers. Many live their whole lives

never realizing they are Star Touched. These beings light up the world with their radiance.

The Innkeeper—Miriam's husband, he seems a fair enough man.

The Tundra—The dangerous that surrounds Christmas Land. Vagabonds and others that cannot live peaceably in Christmas Land are sent here. But not all are bad. It is covered in snow more than Christmas Land, with great hills and dense forests it is a dangerous wonderland.

Tundra Elves—The Tundra Elves are a kindly people that for reasons of their own have no desire to live within Christmas Land. They live a wild, sometimes seemingly savage life, in the woods with their animal friends.

Tyrissia [Tie-reese-ia]—A Tundra Elf. She commands more magic that usual for an Elf and is ancient beyond belief. She only wants to ensure the Christmas Star survives and flourishes with life.

Acknowledgements

I never thought this book would ever be finished.

Good thing I was wrong.

My parents introduced me to books the day I was born and from there a love for all things fiction took off.

I would like to thank my family for their support. They stood behind me throughout the entire process of writing. They helped me wade through my first sorry attempts at this book and read the first draft that sounded like an old shoe brought to life.

All their support meant the world to me.

Thanks.

About The Author

Marcel Ortiz lives in Scio, Oregon with her family and her persnickety animals on their farm.

When she's not writing or going to school she plays basketball and reads full time. Though sometimes she can't resist getting her hands dirty and helping out around the farm.

Her family is kind enough to put up with her scribbling storylines on important pieces of paper and helps keep her grounded in the real world.

She plans to continue to write far into the future, creating new worlds.

Made in the USA
Charleston, SC
08 December 2012